"I… Ben…" she said, frowning, because she had no idea what to say.

Her first instinct had been to protest his overfamiliarity, because it was completely inappropriate.

But that was the response of Princess Amelia Moretti, who always had to be conscious of her reputation, and how she was perceived by the public. There was no such requirement here.

"We shouldn't," she said, but then her hand lifted, bunched in his shirt, her eyes hooked to his, begging, willing him to kiss her. Full lips parted on a sigh, a hope, and then, when he didn't move, she leaned forward a little, inviting him more obviously.

"You say we shouldn't with your mouth." His eyes fell to her lips. "And yet your body is suggesting you want something else entirely."

He moved forward, and her heart skipped a beat as she waited to be kissed. But he didn't take her mouth. Instead, it was Amelia who pushed up, heat in her veins, desperation firing through her as she fused her mouth to his and felt as though a thousand lightning bolts were striking through her soul.

The Diamond Club

Billion-dollar secrets behind every door...

Welcome to The Diamond Club: the world's most exclusive society, open only to the ten richest men and women alive. The suites are opulent. The service is flawless. And privacy is paramount! You'll never see the details of these billionaires' blistering romances in any of the papers—but you can read all about them right here!

Baby Worth Billions by Lynne Graham

Pregnant Princess Bride by Caitlin Crews

Greek's Forbidden Temptation by Millie Adams

Italian's Stolen Wife by Lorraine Hall

Heir Ultimatum by Michelle Smart

His Runaway Royal by Clare Connelly

Reclaimed with a Ring by Louise Fuller

Stranded and Seduced by Emmy Grayson

All available now!

HIS RUNAWAY ROYAL

CLARE CONNELLY

Harlequin
PRESENTS

 **Harlequin®**
PRESENTS™

Recycling programs for this product may not exist in your area.

ISBN-13: 978-1-335-93903-6

His Runaway Royal

Copyright © 2024 by Clare Connelly

All rights reserved. No part of this book may be used or reproduced in any manner whatsoever without written permission.

Without limiting the author's and publisher's exclusive rights, any unauthorized use of this publication to train generative artificial intelligence (AI) technologies is expressly prohibited.

This is a work of fiction. Names, characters, places and incidents are either the product of the author's imagination or are used fictitiously. Any resemblance to actual persons, living or dead, businesses, companies, events or locales is entirely coincidental.

For questions and comments about the quality of this book, please contact us at CustomerService@Harlequin.com.

TM and ® are trademarks of Harlequin Enterprises ULC.

 Harlequin Enterprises ULC
22 Adelaide St. West, 41st Floor
Toronto, Ontario M5H 4E3, Canada
www.Harlequin.com

Printed in Lithuania

 **MIX**
Paper | Supporting responsible forestry
FSC® C021394

Clare Connelly was raised in small-town Australia among a family of avid readers. She spent much of her childhood up a tree, Harlequin book in hand. Clare is married to her own real-life hero, and they live in a bungalow near the sea with their two children. She is frequently found staring into space—a surefire sign she is in the world of her characters. She has a penchant for French food and ice-cold champagne, and Harlequin novels continue to be her favorite-ever books. Writing for Harlequin Presents is a long-held dream. Clare can be contacted via clareconnelly.com or on her Facebook page.

Books by Clare Connelly

Harlequin Presents

Emergency Marriage to the Greek
Pregnant Princess in Manhattan
The Boss's Forbidden Assistant
Twelve Nights in the Prince's Bed

Passionately Ever After...

Cinderella in the Billionaire's Castle

The Long-Lost Cortéz Brothers

The Secret She Must Tell the Spaniard
Desert King's Forbidden Temptation

Brooding Billionaire Brothers

The Sicilian's Deal For "I Do"
Contracted and Claimed by the Boss

Visit the Author Profile page
at Harlequin.com for more titles.

PROLOGUE

FINALLY ENSCONCED IN the seclusion of Benedetto di Vassi's exclusive suite in the heart of the opulent, private members' Diamond Club, Benedetto turned to his friend and spoke, his accented voice gravelled courtesy of the lateness of the hour.

'What is it?'

Crown Prince Anton strode to the windows that framed a postcard view of the London street. 'I need a favour.'

'So I gather,' Benedetto responded, voice droll, but inside he acknowledged that whatever Anton asked of him, he would agree to, for the simple reason that Anton had stood by him through everything that had happened—had been at his side in the worst days of grief, had supported him when Benedetto would have given up entirely.

There was *nothing* he wouldn't do for the man.

'It's Amelia.'

Benedetto knew all about the spoiled younger sister of the Catarno royal family—the Runaway Royal, as she'd been dubbed in the media, because she'd simply woken up one day and decided to abdicate all of her royal duties—and responsibilities to her family—and disappear.

'Go on.'

Anton paused as the door opened and one of the club

stewards entered with a silver tray atop which sat a pair of whisky glasses. Both men waited silently for them to be placed on a nearby table.

Though the staff at the club signed strict confidentiality agreements, neither Anton nor Benedetto saw discretion as optional.

'I need her to come home.'

Benedetto moved to the whisky, lifted both glasses, carried one to his friend.

'The wedding is in two weeks. Already the media is in a frenzy about whether or not she'll be attending—it's all they can focus on.' Frustration was obvious in Anton's features. 'This day is supposed to be joyous. Vanessa deserves that much, doesn't she?' he asked, his eyes lightening as he spoke of his fiancée.

'Yes, she deserves that,' Benedetto agreed, finding it impossible to keep the censure from his tone when he thought of the spoiled princess Amelia. What a brat she was, not only to have run away in the first place, but also to have stayed away even as the wedding of her oldest brother, and the heir to the throne, approached.

'Frankly, I just need Amelia to come home, wear a pretty dress, stand beside us and smile.'

'Yes,' Benedetto said, because of course that made sense. Otherwise the media would go on about her absence and it would overshadow everything else. 'And she's said no?'

Anton nodded. 'She said it's best if she stays away. I know the media has given her a hard time in the past— she always copped it worse than Rowan and me—but this is really too much.'

Benedetto didn't reply. He wasn't inclined to cut Amelia any slack. After all, the media was capable of saying or writing whatever they wanted but, at the end of the day, it was just words.

Words only had the power to wound if you ceded that to them; she should have known better. Besides, the glare of the newspapers was nothing compared to the grief of losing a child—until you'd felt that loss and desolation, you didn't understand true suffering.

Everything in Benedetto's life was benchmarked against that pain he'd known and continued to know each and every day of his life.

Until his dying day, he would think of Sasha with an emptiness inside that simply wouldn't quit. It was an emptiness he relished, though. What right did he have to enjoy his life in any way when he hadn't been able to save his beautiful, sweet daughter?

'We've generally taken a policy of allowing Amelia to be Amelia. Let her sort out whatever's going on in her head and come home when she's ready. Of course—' he laughed without humour '—we thought it would be a matter of weeks. Maybe months. But she's now two years into this self-imposed exile with no sign of returning. It's gone too far.' He took a drink of his whisky, winced as the flavour hit the back of his throat. 'My parents are suffering far more than they let on. They miss her. We all do.'

Benedetto kept his own thoughts private from his friend. He'd never met Amelia—most of his time with Anton had been spent abroad, here in London or over in the States, and when he had gone to the small, yet exceptionally wealthy, country of Catarno, he had only met the King and Queen and Anton's brother once. He had, however, heard enough about Amelia, read enough about her, known enough women like her over the years, to have formed a pretty good idea of what she was like.

Nonetheless, she was Anton's sister and he understood the way families and loyalty worked.

'How can I help?'

Anton's relief was visible. 'Would you go to her, Ben? You're the only one I could ever trust with this. I need you to do whatever it takes to bring her home.' He took a step closer to his friend, eyes closed a moment. 'Please.'

The last word was unnecessary—most of the request had been. Benedetto had decided to help from the moment Anton had asked. Determination glinted in the depths of Benedetto's obsidian eyes. 'I'll have her there for the wedding—I promise.'

CHAPTER ONE

BEFORE BOARDING THE yacht Amelia stared east across the sparkling ocean, as she did each and every day—looking towards home. It was a long way away, separated from her by land, sea, miles and too vast an array of problems for Amelia to ever imagine traversing, but that didn't mean she didn't miss it, didn't yearn to be back with all her heart. She could never go home, though—she couldn't risk it.

She narrowed her eyes a little, imagining what her parents were doing, her brothers, imagining the palace she'd grown up in and always loved, with the light sloping in through the fourteenth-century windows. She visualised the gardens at this time of year. Amelia always thought they were prettiest in summer when the fragrance of blossom was heavy in the air, and the roses were abundant.

She imagined walking amongst them, running her hands over the petals, picking one, lifting it to her nose. But when she inhaled from her vantage point, all she caught was the heady tang of sea water and citrus.

This was home now. On the outskirts of Valencia, where she had been able to reinvent herself, to emerge from her pain and shock-induced chrysalis as someone new. Someone independent. Most importantly, someone *not* royal. She might desperately want to go back to the palace and her family but that didn't mean she hadn't also fallen in love with her life here. It was quiet and dull, by most people's standards, but Amelia was not the average twenty-four-year-old. She'd been to more than enough parties, balls and overseas holidays to last a lifetime. Now she was very happy to simply exist.

Perhaps she hadn't emerged from her chrysalis after all? These could well be indications of still being in a state of retreat, of desperately needing to heal from her shock and heartbreak, from the deep sense of betrayal that had made her withdraw from the world.

A seagull flew overhead, dipping low towards the ocean, scouring with great talent and experience, minimal effort expended in a wide-span glide until the perfect moment, when the bird dived straight down, half disappearing into the ocean and emerging victoriously only seconds later with a small fish in its beak. A natural predator. The fish swimming just beneath the surface hadn't stood a chance when the bird had decided to strike. Poor defenceless fish!

Amelia grimaced wistfully, pulled on the strap of her backpack and began to move again, away from the pretty wildness of the beach towards the pristine, perfectly maintained marina, where almost all of the boats were pleasure crafts—though she was gratified to see a handful of working fishing boats still amongst them.

But, more and more, this had become a place of wealth and luxury, and the marina reflected that. Amongst the impressive yachts, one in particular stood out. A sixth sense alerted her that it would be the boat she was looking for without even needing to read the name, but as she approached, the words *Il Galassia* caught her eye.

Bingo, she thought.

Her experience in real-estate photography was relatively limited, though she'd received positive feedback from her clients and enjoyed the work. She'd been hired through her agency to capture high-end apartments and homes prior to sale, and she'd thrived at that task. A yacht, though, was something new, different from the standard homes she'd been photographing.

She'd always loved the water. As a girl, she'd summered aboard the royal yacht, and handsome naval officers had served as crew, teaching Amelia all about the operations with good humour and answering her millions of questions without even a hint of impatience.

She stilled exactly where she was, noting the way the afternoon sun caught the glistening white of the mega yacht, and her fingers twitched. Without another moment's hesitation, she removed her backpack and lifted out the camera, bringing it to her face and looking through the lens as she shifted it slightly, until the sunbeams seemed almost to cut through the bow, and then she adjusted the focus, took a deep breath and clicked.

For Amelia, photography was an almost spiritual act. It always had been. Capturing a moment, a memory, seemed kind of magical. But ever since leaving behind everyone she knew and loved, all the places that had until a few years ago defined her, Amelia hadn't understood quite how important her photos would be, for they were reminders of what she'd walked away from, what she'd cared enough about saving to sacrifice from her life.

She held the camera out so she could see the image, and flashed a quick smile of satisfaction, with no concept of the man behind one of the many tinted windows of the yacht, looking out at her with a disapproving scowl on his face.

* * *

To Benedetto di Vassi, Princess Amelia looked exactly as he'd thought she would: very beautiful, almost hauntingly so, with her slender, willowy figure and long, waving blonde hair pulled into a loose braid that fell with the appearance of carelessness over one shoulder. Her skin was a deep tan, a colour that spoke of much time spent sunbathing for the sake of vanity, and her dress was floaty, like something from the seventies—falling to her ankles, revealing brown leather sandals. It was as though she'd just stepped off a photoshoot—she was the last word in beach chic. The only concession to her profession was the backpack she wore, from which she'd just removed a camera.

Lips tightening into a line on his handsome face, Benedetto pushed away from the window, rubbing a hand over his chin.

He'd agreed to help Anton and he didn't regret it, but he wasn't a total Neanderthal. The idea of kidnapping a woman wasn't something he relished. Nor was he thrilled about involving his staff in the whole business, so he'd carefully selected only his two most trusted team members: Cassidy and Christopher. Between them, they'd pilot the yacht, take care of the housekeeping duties, cooking, cleaning, anything that was needed. But it didn't matter how comfortable he made the princess for this voyage.

At the end of the day, he was taking her liberty.

He was taking her back home.

And given that she'd spent the last couple of years assiduously disappearing into obscurity, it was natural to presume she wouldn't be thrilled.

His loyalty was not to Amelia, though. It was Anton he owed everything to, Anton he had promised to help. No matter what.

'Cassidy, you said?'

'Yeah.' The woman's accent was Australian. She had hair that was only a slightly darker brown than her skin, and her eyes were mesmerisingly beautiful. She grinned, revealing perfect white teeth. 'Ben's waiting for you.'

Amelia raised a brow, feasting on the details of the yacht.

Her agent hadn't specified how many pictures would be needed, so, as with any listing, Amelia figured she'd take an abundance and work it out later. There was certainly no shortage of stunning angles. The yacht looked to be almost brand new—she wondered what could have happened to require its sale.

'Is Ben the sales agent?' Amelia asked, falling into step beside the other woman.

'Nah, he's the owner.'

'Oh.' Amelia frowned. Her agent hadn't mentioned that the owner would be on board. Usually, the residences she photographed were empty, giving Amelia the run of the place, and she preferred it that way. She'd been drawn to real-estate photography particularly because it was a solitary task, with little interaction required with anyone besides her agent. A friend of a friend, he always respected her boundaries, never pushed her about her other life.

'Well, I'll try to stay out of his way.'

'That won't be necessary,' a man said. His voice was deep and rough, and as he spoke a summer breeze rustled past them, so Amelia's hair brushed her cheek and she felt as though his voice had somehow transformed into a caress, the lightest of touches. She shivered, turned without meaning to, bracing herself, though she couldn't have said why she felt that was necessary.

Electricity flooded the very air around them, the summer breeze morphing into a fierce storm in which Amelia was caught.

She hadn't expected to meet anyone on board the yacht except perhaps the crew, and she certainly hadn't expected to meet anyone like this.

Casting about, she tried to rationalise her reaction, to understand what it was about the man that was so immediately unsettling, so threatening. Physically, he was obviously very strong, with broad shoulders and a toned abdomen hinted at by the white business shirt he wore, making her mouth weirdly dry. He wore chinos, a caramel-brown colour, with a dark brown belt, but his feet were bare—an odd discrepancy with the rest of his formal outfit. Amelia tried to swallow but a lump had formed that made it difficult.

Jerking her attention back to his face, she catalogued everything she saw there with what she told herself was a photographer's interest: the symmetry of his features, strong, harsh, angular yet somehow incredibly compelling, as though he had secrets to tell, and she was suddenly desperate to hear them. His jaw was square, belying an inner strength that was further conveyed by the harsh set of his lips. But it was his eyes that threatened to turn her knees to jelly. They were almost jet-black, and *fierce*. It was the only word she could think of. They radiated an intense anger, an emotion that made no sense, and yet she was sure he was looking at her as though…

But then he blinked, and his eyes softened, just enough to make her doubt her first, silly interpretations.

How long did they stand there, neither speaking? What was he thinking about her? Had he been looking at her the way she had him? Amelia had been so caught up in her own inspection she hadn't noticed, but surely one of them needed to say something. The electricity in the air arced and sizzled. Amelia felt parched and over-warm.

'This is the photographer,' Cassidy interjected in her cheery Australian voice. 'Millie, right?'

Grateful to have someone else there to cut through the strange vortex of tension, Amelia cast her glance sideways. Hearing the diminutive version of her name, that she'd used since leaving home, was slightly mollifying. 'Yes, right. Millie.'

'This is Ben, and this beautiful thing is his.' Cassidy ran her hand over the railing of the boat, then turned back to Ben. 'I was just going to give Millie a tour.'

Ben shook his head. 'I'll do it.'

Amelia's insides clenched. She wasn't sure if she was happy with that pronouncement, or filled with dread, but her whole body seemed to react to his statement in an alarming way. Heat flooded her veins, and her fingers shook, so she clasped them together in front of herself.

Cassidy left quickly, with one last look in Amelia's direction—an expression of apology. Had she seen the anger on Ben's face too? Was he a grumpy person, habitually, and was Cassidy regretting the necessity of leaving them alone together?

Amelia's mouth pulled to the side, her eyes shifting quickly to the gangplank, wondering how bad it would be for her career if she were to quickly abscond.

Strictly speaking, she didn't need the money.

She had a trust fund that had come through her mother's family, nothing to do with the royal lineage. She had accessed it only since leaving the palace, to buy a small apartment, and any of the necessities absolutely required. But the thrill of earning her own money had caught Amelia by surprise. The pay was hardly extravagant, and yet it was all hers, accrued through her hard work and skill, and she'd become addicted to that.

There was no way she could turn her back on this commission, even when there was something about the owner of the boat that set her nerves on edge.

'Let me show you the entertaining spaces first.'

Amelia's instincts went into overdrive, but she ignored them with effort.

'Lead the way.' She spoke, finally, realising that, apart from confirming her name, she had yet to offer any intelligible words. Her voice sounded prim to her own ears, formal, driven back to the comfort and familiarity of the persona she'd adopted when forced to attend state events. She attempted to soften the words with a smile, but even that felt tight. She looked away instead, giving up.

Impressing him wasn't part of her job description. She was there to take photos, nothing more.

And yet, as he led the way to a wide set of doors, she was aware of him on a soul-deep level. Every step he took, even his inhalations, seemed almost as though they were her own. The hairs on the back of her neck were standing, and her stomach felt as if it were rolling around in a washing machine.

'This is one of the lounge areas,' he said, apparently unaware of the tension eddies assaulting Amelia from the inside out. She did her best to focus on the tour instead, regarding the space with a trained eye. Perhaps if she'd been less exposed to wealth and luxury, she might have been overawed by the sheer opulence of this room, but Amelia had known such extravagance all her life and so barely gave it a second thought. She shifted her backpack from a shoulder to her hand, unzipping it and removing her camera with an easy grace, too focused on her job to notice how he was looking at her, the way his eyes lingered on her bare shoulder with its faint pink line from the backpack.

When she turned to face him, his gaze had returned to her face, his eyes narrowed analytically, as though he was waiting for her to speak, so she nodded. 'It's very nice.'

Nice was a bland way to describe the beauty of the room, which was large and expansive, furnished in cream leather, pale Scandinavian-style minimalist decor, with timber floorboards leading the eye towards the enormous wall of windows offering a breathtaking view of the water from this side, and the marina on the other.

It was stunning, and yet, somehow, she wasn't sure it felt like what she imagined this man would choose. She barely knew him, but her first impression had been of someone quite wild and untamed, someone virile and overtly masculine. So what? she thought, hiding a smile by tilting her head. Had she expected black leather and animal prints?

'You are amused?'

Damn it. She grimaced inwardly, composed her features, then turned to him with an expression of wide-eyed innocence. 'Not at all. Shall I start here?' She lifted her camera, to remind them both of her reason for being in his private space.

'Let me show you the rest of the boat first, then you can decide.'

'Okay.' She shrugged, her mouth drying as his eyes dropped from her face to one of her shoulders, lingering there just long enough for her skin to respond by lifting in goosebumps. Shockingly to Amelia, in addition to that visible response, she experienced the unfamiliar sensation of her nipples tingling almost painfully, hardening against the soft cotton of her dress—she wore no bra. Life in Valencia was warm and free. Besides, Amelia hadn't been endowed with the kind of figure that required restraint. How often she'd looked at her curvier friends and wished, more than anything, that she'd been the recipient of well-rounded breasts. Alas, it was not her lot in life to set the world on fire with spectacular cleavage. 'You're such a clothes horse, you lucky thing,' her mother had remarked on multiple occasions, probably trying to make Amelia feel good about her naturally slender frame.

Now she wished for the protective armour of a bra, or ten of the things, as her whole body seemed to come alive as though being licked by flames, white-hot and destructive.

She turned away from him, breath snagging in her throat so her voice emerged breathy and light. 'Where to next?'

'Well, not that way,' he drawled, sardonic amusement in his tone. 'Unless you are planning a swim.'

Her eyes focused beyond the wall of glass on a pool, spectacularly aquamarine, with the appearance of disappearing out into the ocean. Now *that* she was impressed by.

'It does look inviting,' she murmured truthfully, as heat threatened to send her pulse haywire.

'Another time, perhaps,' he responded, so she immediately snapped herself out of it.

Another time?

No. Amelia shut the thought down instantly. There would be no other time.

For as determined as she was to escape her past, she knew that meant limiting her exposure in the present. She missed her friends, and there were times when she was unspeakably lonely, but this was the life she'd chosen for herself. It was the way it had to be. She could never risk getting close to anyone again. Not after what had happened. How could she ever trust anyone again, after her boyfriend had betrayed her, had blackmailed her with revealing Amelia's most personal secret?

Although, it wasn't really *her* secret.

She was the by-product of it, the evidence, but it was her mother who'd cheated, and fallen pregnant to someone other than the King. Her mother who'd conceived Amelia outside the marital bed, who'd lied to all and sundry about Amelia's parentage. It was her mother who'd foisted Amelia upon the royal family, who'd raised her to believe her father a man who was no such thing, who'd raised Amelia to see her brothers as that, rather than half-brothers, who would likely disown her if they knew the truth.

It was for the Queen, her mother's sake, that she'd run away.

And also King Timothy, the man who'd raised her, for if he learned the truth it would surely destroy him.

Tears threatened to spark in Amelia's eyes and she blinked rapidly to forestall them. Of all the times to let her life story seep into her present, this was not it. She dragged practised defences around herself like a wall of steel.

'Have you organised with the realtor to send someone for the floor plan?' Her voice wobbled a little. She cleared her throat, dug her nails into her palm and tried again. 'Then again, the yacht looks very new, so perhaps you have one from construction?'

'I do,' he confirmed, with no mention of the emotion in her voice. She was glad. Much like when you fell over and the worst thing a bystander could do was ask if you were okay, she didn't want him to check on her, as she feared she might weaken and confess that she wasn't. Why now? Why this man?

She blinked quickly, assumed a businesslike expression. 'Lead the way, Mr...?' She let the question hang in the air between them.

He was quiet, thoughtful. Too thoughtful for such a simple query, but, a moment later, answered. 'Di Vassi. Benedetto di Vassi.'

'Di Vassi,' she murmured, wondering why the name was familiar to her. It was an unusual surname and yet she was sure she'd heard it before. 'Have we met?'

'No,' he said with easy confidence, and so she believed him, yet the slight warning bell dinging in the back of her mind didn't ease up, even as he led her into yet another opulent living space, this time with a large dining table and bar. The next room showed a grand piano and several leather sofas. Finally, there was a room that was both a library and office, a timber desk in the middle of the room, a floor-to-ceiling window revealing more stunning views of the ocean, and a wall that was lined with books. As a bibliophile from way back, Amelia itched to move closer to the shelves and scan the spines, but there'd be time for that later, once he'd finished the tour and she was exploring on her own.

They stepped into a corridor. Several doors were shut on the other side.

'Bedrooms,' he said. 'Shall we?'

But her body revolted at the idea. She was terrified of the very notion of being in a bedroom with this man when her pulse was going crazy and her insides were a melting pot of awareness.

'Later,' she managed to say.

'Fine. Come downstairs, then.'

Was she imagining the hesitation in his voice? The hint of emotion?

Her feet wouldn't shift. She remained where she was, planted in the middle of the hallway, so when he stepped forward to lead her to the wide staircase, Amelia still didn't move, and their bodies were brought within a couple of inches of each other. She caught a hint of his fragrance— masculine, pine and pepper, spicy and seductive—and she closed her eyes as a wave of desire, unmistakable and powerful, washed over her. Her lips parted as she tried to process these feelings, to understand why they should be besieging her here, now, of all places.

'I—perhaps I should finish looking around on my own,' she suggested haltingly, self-preservation driving the suggestion because, inwardly, what she wanted most of all was more time with this man, whom she found unspeakably compelling.

'For what reason?' he asked, and stepped forward once more, so their bodies were now almost touching.

She let out a soft groan, because she felt as though she were fighting a losing battle. When had she last been kissed? Touched? Looked at with longing?

That was easy to answer. She'd broken up with Daniel a week before leaving Catarno. It had been the beginning of the worst week of her life, and ever since, she'd avoided men like the plague. But even before their breakup, it hadn't been a passionate relationship. They'd fallen in love slowly and safely, which had only made his betrayal worse. He'd been her friend first, and then he'd used her for financial gain.

This was all overpowering, and, to Amelia's surprise, she found she *liked* the way it felt to be overcome by attraction, even when it was simultaneously terrifying.

What would happen if she gave into temptation? If she lifted up onto the tips of her toes—even though she was quite tall, he was taller still, by several inches—and kissed him? Would he be shocked? Or was he as attracted to her as she was to him?

Somewhere, far away from Amelia and the fantasy world she'd begun to inhabit, she was aware of a soft rumbling sound, a feeling that made her legs vibrate a little beneath her. Or was that yet another indication of her attraction to this man?

His eyes flared, as if she'd spoken the thought aloud, and then he lifted a hand, large and capable, fingers dark with short nails, and took hold of her face. Not gently, not even sensually. This was a touch of possession and curiosity, as though he had every right, and she was reminded of how he'd looked at her on the deck, the anger in his eyes, and she wondered if that same emotion was driving his touch now.

But then he expelled a long, slow breath, warm against her temples, and his gaze narrowed as if he was confused. 'Your eyes are so different.'

She blinked, not understanding. 'From what?'

Something must have happened to cause the water beneath them to roll—perhaps another large boat departing the marina—because she lost her balance a little, and it took Benedetto's hand reaching out to steady her. It was quickly done, a clinical touch at first, but then with another, faster, rougher breath, he shifted the hand from her arm to her hip, then around her back, pressing her forward with the same easy command as he'd touched her face seconds earlier.

'I— Ben—' she said, frowning, because she had no idea what to say. Her first instinct had been to protest his over-familiarity, because it was completely inappropriate.

But that was the response of Princess Amelia Moretti, who always had to be conscious of her reputation, and how she was perceived by the public. There was no such requirement here. But still, how could she trust him not to betray her if she gave into this? How could she ever trust anyone? The saving grace was that he didn't know who she was. To him, she was just a photographer, not a princess with a small fortune at her fingertips.

His hand at her back moved lower, to the dip above her bottom, and his fingers were splayed wide, moving slowly, hypnotically, seductively, so she struggled to make sense of anything.

'What do you want?' he asked, rough, deep.

Amelia was totally swept away, and yet there was a small part of her brain capable of rational thought and in it she marvelled at this sudden strange turn of events. She'd never been the kind of woman to go for strong-man types, yet here she was, desperate to strip naked and make love to a man who was really more beast than anything else.

'I—shouldn't—'

His smile was mocking. God, he was insufferable. 'You shouldn't?' he prompted, and now when he stepped forward, he pulled her with him, or rather shifted her, so her back pressed against the wall of the corridor, and his body formed an equally hard frame, one hand pressed to the wall beside her head, the other still on her face. His knee, somehow, had come between her legs, and she thanked heaven for that because without the support she wasn't sure she could stand upright. And yet, she found herself dying to press lower against him, to rub her sex against his skin, and her cheeks flushed a deep pink at the very X-rated direction of her thoughts.

'We shouldn't,' she said, but then her hand lifted, bunched in his shirt, her eyes hooked to his, begging, willing him to kiss her. Full lips parted on a sigh, a hope, and then, when he didn't move, she leaned forward a little, inviting him more obviously.

'You say we shouldn't with your mouth...' his eyes fell to that part of her body '...and yet your body is suggesting you want something else entirely.'

He was right. She was sending mixed messages. But that wasn't Amelia's fault. Her brain was completely scrambled.

'Saying we shouldn't doesn't mean I don't want to,' she said honestly, a moment later, the confession whispered. 'Does that make sense?'

'You have no idea how much sense,' he admitted darkly, eyes flashing to hers as he moved forward, and her heart skipped a beat as she waited to be kissed. But he didn't take her mouth. Instead, it was Amelia who pushed up, heat in her veins, desperation firing through her as she fused her mouth to his and felt as though a thousand lightning bolts were striking through her soul.

She hadn't known what to expect...but it wasn't this. Her whole body rejoiced at the contact, her mouth exploring his with passionate hunger and need, her hands roaming his body possessively, from his arms to his shoulders to his nape, tangling in the hair there, so her breasts were crushed to his chest. He made a noise low in his throat and Amelia felt as though she might almost lose consciousness. It was a kiss that managed to throw everything from her mind, all thought and knowledge dissipated in the face of such an onslaught of white-hot passion, and Amelia could not have cared less.

CHAPTER TWO

THIS HAD *NOT* been a part of the plan. Not exactly. He'd known he would need to distract her, as the boat left the marina, and he hadn't worked out how. Their clear mutual attraction had caught him off guard. Capitalising on it was an easy solution, but it was more than that. He *wanted* to kiss her. He *wanted* all of her, and he was totally blind-sided by that.

Hell, this was his best friend's younger sister. A woman he despised, a spoilt, selfish brat he'd been begged to bring home with her tail between her legs. At no point had he considered seducing her, or being seduced by her, so what the hell was happening?

Just because something shouldn't happen it doesn't mean you don't want it to.

Damn straight.

But Benedetto was no inexperienced teenager. He was a man well into his thirties, who'd lived a full life in all aspects, and had plenty of relationships to have learned from. He didn't need to slake his libido with Princess Amelia. There were dozens of women he could call on for that, if and when he decided he was in the mood. So what the hell was he doing? There were other ways to distract her; he didn't need to do this—and yet he couldn't stop.

She moaned again, this time louder, and rolled her hips, her body imploring him to do something more than just taste her, and before he realised what he was doing, his hands moved roughly, impatient now for what he'd wanted the moment she'd strolled onto the boat, a picture of casual summer beauty. He'd seen enough photographs of Amelia, and it had never occurred to him to be attracted to her. She was in every way off limits to him.

But he'd never actually met her.

And despite the experience that should have inured him to this kind of attraction, it had also taught him to respect the laws of chemistry. Sometimes, you just couldn't fight it.

Besides, the Crown Prince had told Benedetto to bring Amelia home, whatever it took. Okay, Anton wouldn't have had this in mind, but Benedetto wasn't going to fail his friend.

Acknowledging, in the back of his mind, that he was simply making excuses to justify his weakness, he nonetheless allowed himself to succumb to temptation, figuring he'd sort out the consequences later. After.

'Are you sure we don't know each other?' she asked, huskily, momentarily piercing his fog of desire.

'We've never met,' he responded, though it didn't quite answer her question. She'd clearly recognised his name—undoubtedly her brother had mentioned him at some point over the years. But theirs was not a personal connection. Or at least, it hadn't been.

'Okay.' She tilted her head back, giving him better access to her throat, and he took it without hesitation. Now it was Benedetto's turn to groan as he brushed his stubble over her skin, so soft it was like velvet, feeling her purr.

Her dress was simple—elasticised across the torso in a

style a woman would probably know the name of—with no straps, so it was the easiest thing in the world for him to tug at the side and lower it. She gasped as he revealed one of her perfect, neat breasts, the darkened areola taut and firm, so he was drawn like a moth to a flame to pull the nipple into his mouth and suck on it, harder perhaps than he'd intended, so she bucked against his leg in surprise, her whole body jerking with the strength of her physical response.

'Do you want me to stop?' he asked, dark anger in his voice—an anger that was directed at himself, for having insufficient willpower.

She shook her head quickly, but her eyes were huge, a look of awakening in them that had him briefly questioning her experience with men. 'You're not a virgin, are you?' After all, he had to draw the line somewhere, and he had no interest in being Anton's sister's first sexual experience.

She shook her head again and relief surged through him.

'But I'm— I haven't—' She grimaced. 'Never mind.'

He did as she requested, thrusting aside whatever she'd been about to say and instead giving himself full access to her body, pulling the dress down on the other side so he could lose himself in her breasts, her nipples, exploring them hungrily with his mouth and then his hands, enjoying the way her pupils dilated when he squeezed her nipples as he rolled them, the way she bit down on her lip as he palmed her breasts, her hands desperately running over her body when he pulled away, as though she were on fire and needed extinguishing.

It was all getting away from him.

He should stop this. The boat had to be out of the marina by now. She was his ward for the next week, the time it would take to sail to Catarno. He had to take control of the situation. Didn't he?

'Please,' she whimpered, the fire raging out of control. He understood; he felt it too.

'Please what?'

'What do you mean?'

'What do you want from me, Amelia?' he demanded, eyes latched to hers, so he saw something shift in them, a frown tugging on her lips.

'I want—what did you call me?'

His heart thumped against his chest as he belatedly realised his mistake. He'd used her christened name, rather than what she went by now.

Pride stopped him from lying. His arousal was straining hard against his trousers, his whole body was taut with need, and yet he stood straight, dropped his hands to his sides and regarded her as though nothing had happened between them whatsoever. Even when desire was threatening to turn him to mush, making him want to forget everyone and everything but her, he held onto sanity just long enough to know he couldn't lie to her. Not when asked a direct question.

'It is your name, *si*?'

She flinched, confusion and betrayal writ large across her face. 'We *have* met,' she said, lifting her fingers to her lips. 'You know who I am.'

She was so shocked she didn't even think to draw her dress back up, so Benedetto had the vantage point of her feminine form, mottled pink by his stubble and the desperate need of his touch.

'No,' he said, crossing his arms over his chest simply

to stop himself from reaching for her. She looked so hurt, so crestfallen, it was impossible not to feel sorry for her.

Benedetto had to remind himself of everything he knew about Amelia: her spoiled, overindulged ways, the only daughter of parents who doted on her, the fact she'd cast her family aside and disappeared into the ether, hurtfully ignoring almost all their attempts at contact. He hated women like her, who had no loyalty nor respect for other people. 'And yes,' he finished, interested in her reaction.

Her eyes swept shut, her lips parted, and her features were so defeated, her expression so haunted, it was impossible not to experience an overarching sense of compunction for his place in all of it.

'Why? How did you find me?'

'You are not so well hidden away, Princess,' he responded.

He'd never been into role play but apparently when it was a real-life princess that was a different matter. Out of nowhere, he had an image of her in a palace, and he her concubine, existing purely to service her needs, and felt a thrill of something that surprised him. Benedetto had never needed a woman for longer than it suited him. He'd never really been wired to seek relationships, but after those awful days of grief and loss, he'd known he wouldn't again risk that kind of pain—nor emotional connection. He didn't deserve it.

'So what was all this?' She gestured to the boat and then, belatedly realising she was half naked, she pulled up her dress, shielding herself from his view so he wanted to cry out in objection, to reach forward and remove the dress altogether. 'Why am I here?' she demanded, and then her eyes widened as she looked around, lifted a hand to her lips. 'Oh, my God. The boat's moving, isn't it? Why is the boat moving?'

'Because we're leaving port,' he responded simply. He was angry with her for what she'd put her family through, so he'd thought he'd enjoy this moment, but the truth was Benedetto felt as though he was speaking words that were at odds with how he should be acting. He'd committed to this path though; he had to follow through. Besides, he'd run the plan briefly via Anton, who'd said only that she had to be brought home.

'We can deal with her anger when she's back in Catarno.'

And so here Benedetto was, a tool of the palace. This wasn't his fight, and it wasn't his business. He was simply doing as he'd been asked by the one person he could never say no to.

'You're kidnapping me,' she said quietly, shaking like a leaf. 'Oh, my God.'

'No.'

But it was obvious she didn't believe him. 'You're kidnapping me,' she said again. 'At least have the decency to be honest about it.' She was clearly terrified and yet she still had such strength and dignity.

'I am not kidnapping you,' he said, then frowned. Because wasn't that exactly what he was doing? 'At least, not for any nefarious reason. You can relax, Princess.'

'Oh, gee, can I?'

'All I am doing is taking you home.'

It was as if he'd said he planned to kill her. She paled before his eyes, her skin losing any hint of a tan, even her lips draining of colour, so he reached forward on instinct alone, because it was clear what was about to happen. Sure enough, she collapsed the second his arms connected with her body, her frame going limp, and a thousand memories jolted through him.

Memories of Sasha slammed into him hard, so his own skin paled, his heart raced, his palms felt sweaty as remembered trauma flooded his body. And yet, just as he had then, he pushed past those feelings to act as was necessary, scooping Amelia up against his chest and carrying her, watching her face—but this wasn't a seizure, not as Sash used to experience. This was different. Amelia had fainted from shock. He didn't need to worry that she was going to swallow her tongue, that she was going to die because he wasn't paying attention.

Nonetheless, the memories of his daughter in that last year were an indelible part of his being, haunting him mercilessly. He laid Amelia down on the cream sofa, staring at her with an overwhelming sense of regret, guilt, anger and frustration, pressing a hand against her forehead, then moving it to her arm. So warm, so vital.

She wasn't dying.

He slowed his breathing, focused on the moment, on becoming himself again, on getting rid of the anxiety that was plaguing him, so that when Amelia blinked her eyes open, she'd see no vestige of emotional ache on his features—it was a pain he never intended to show anyone but Anton, who'd been there through the worst of it with him.

Amelia felt as though she were coming to the surface of the water from a long, long way down, the depth of the ocean almost overwhelming, so she struggled to breathe, to think, to see. Her eyes opened and everything swirled in front of her, nothing making sense. Where was she? And who was that?

She scrambled to a seated position, then wished she hadn't when her head began to spin again.

Benedetto stood watchful but unmoving, arms crossed, eyes on her as if held by some invisible force.

'I'm not going home,' she said quickly, the last few moments clarifying in her mind, his words reverberating inside her brain. 'And you cannot make me.'

His lips curled derisively. 'Want to bet?'

'You can't be serious?'

He lifted one shoulder, one beautiful, broad, strong shoulder, so Amelia's mind scattered in a direction she most definitely wouldn't allow it to go.

'Anton is getting married. Your presence is required.'

'I think you mean requested,' she replied with the appearance of calm, when her insides were jangling all over the place. 'And I've already told my family that I cannot make it.'

'You misunderstand. Your attendance is not optional.'

She ground her teeth together, wondering why her body was trembling with something other than anger and fear. Why did she find his awful bossiness…sexy? It was more of that horrid caveman behaviour, which Amelia found abhorrent. Didn't she?

'I'm sorry, since when did you become the boss of me?' she responded with saccharine sweetness, moving to stand.

But he was quicker, closing the space between them and pressing a hand to her shoulder. 'Stay there. I don't particularly want you to pass out again.'

'Thanks for the concern,' she muttered sarcastically. 'But I'll be fine.'

'Maybe, maybe not. Stay where you are.'

It wasn't just that she was angry, she was spoiling for a

fight. He'd stirred up a frenetic energy inside Amelia and all she wanted was to expel it *somehow*. If that was by fighting with him, then so be it.

So she stood up, and pushed at his chest, a thrill of pleasure running through her at how good it felt to take out her annoyance on the man who'd caused it. 'Stop telling me what to do.'

'It's for your own good.'

'Oh, yeah, right, and you're what, a doctor?' she prompted sceptically. 'Some kind of fainting expert?'

His lips clenched. 'Fine, have it your way,' he said, a strange quality to his voice. 'But don't expect me to catch you next time.'

'I didn't expect you to catch me this time,' she responded firmly.

'That doesn't sound like "thank you".'

'You seriously expect me to thank you? I fainted out of shock, a shock caused by your pronouncement that you're attempting to kidnap me against my wishes and return me home, also very much against my wishes. Tell me, what exactly should I be grateful to you for?'

'Kidnapping is, I think, always against a person's wishes,' he said, concentrating on the semantics of her accusation, earning an eye roll from Amelia.

'By all means, correct my sentence structure,' she snapped. 'But that doesn't change the fact you've broken about a million laws. You do realise I'm under the protection of the Catarno royal guard?'

'Are you?' he replied. 'Where are they?'

She floundered. Damn it, that was an easy lie to catch her in. 'I mean, in theory,' she responded testily. 'I have no need for them here, but what you're doing is a serious crime in Catarno. You'd be stupid to take me there and not expect consequences for this.'

'Fine, I'll drop you off just outside the waters of your country,' he said with something like amusement, which only served to strengthen her anger.

'You will do no such thing.' She drew herself up to her full height, no idea that she looked like a modern-day Boudicca with her hair wild around her shoulders and a quiet, dignified strength emanating from her.

'No?'

She shook her head. 'You will have your crew turn this boat around and put it back into dock. I will leave, and never see you again.'

His laugh was a short, sharp sound, filled with the same anger she'd detected in him at their first meeting. 'No.'

'No?' Her nostrils flared. 'What do you mean "no"?'

'Your brother asked me to bring you home, and that's what I'm doing.' She blanched once more, and, despite what he'd said minutes ago, he moved swiftly, as if anticipating the worst, but stopped short of touching her.

'This is absolutely *not* simple,' she said, hands on hips, staring across at him. 'Did it occur to you that I left Catarno for a reason?'

'I presume you had reasons you thought were valid at the time. Perhaps you didn't realise how hard it would be on your family. Or perhaps you just didn't care about them. Maybe you're only capable of caring about yourself and your own happiness,' he added, eyes lancing hers with an accusation that made the bottom fall out of her world.

Was that really what he thought of her?

And had he formed that opinion based on what Anton had disclosed? Was that how Anton viewed her? Nausea flooded Amelia's body, so she spun away to conceal the way her throat moved and her mouth tightened.

'It's none of your business,' she said unevenly, after a long, pained pause. 'I left. I'm a free person, capable of making my own decisions. None of that is your concern.'

'No,' he agreed quickly, so she was gratified. 'And yet, you're hurting someone I owe a huge debt of gratitude to, someone who wants—needs—you to return to Catarno, for one week only.'

'You really think I can go home for a week, attend the wedding, then disappear into my life again? Do you have any idea how impossible that will be? Escaping once was a goddamned miracle, there's no way I'll be able to do it again.'

'Escaping?' He homed in on her use of the word. 'What exactly did you need to escape? A life of idle luxury? Of low expectations and a schedule that was one hundred per cent geared to pleasure-seeking?'

Amelia gasped, shocked by the level of her anger, and by the hand that lifted and struck his cheek, by how good it felt to slap him, to release that tension, shocked by the way his flesh changed colour, darkening red in the shape of her palm, and at the way her stomach knotted—and not from tension so much as something infinitely darker and more dangerous. Shocked and delighted at how he gripped her wrist the moment after she'd connected with his skin, the way his fingers curled around her, held her hand in the air, so much stronger than she was, so easily able to command her body with his.

'Did that feel good?' he asked, eyes like lasers, cutting through her.

'Yes.' She didn't bother to lie. 'It felt bloody great, actually,' she admitted, even when she knew she should feel ashamed. She'd never condoned violence, and it didn't matter that she was his physical inferior, much slighter and weaker, it was still violence. It was still wrong.

His eyes flared, and heat arced between them, so despite her hatred for him, her fear at the thought of going home, that same heady throb of need was tormenting her, making it almost impossible to remember where she was, with whom, and why she had to fight this.

'Do you want to hit me again?' His thumb stroked the flesh of her inner wrist.

She shook her head, confused.

'Don't you?'

'I don't know what I want.'

His eyes flared at the unintentionally provocative comment. 'You're angry with me.'

'Do you blame me?'

His lip contorted into something like a half-smile, but it was rich with sardonic mockery.

'What I don't understand,' she continued, 'is why *you're* angry with *me*?' Her pulse quickened, her body so close to his, the hand on her wrist too benign to explain the impact his proximity was having.

'What makes you say that I am angry?'

'I can tell.'

'Are you a mind-reader?'

'Don't do that,' she murmured.

'Do what?'

'Gaslight me. I know what I feel from you, and it's anger.'

'Yes,' he admitted, though she saw surprise in his features, and something like grudging respect. 'Fine, I am angry with you too.'

'Why?'

'Because of what you have put your family through. Because of how careless and selfish you have been.'

There it was again! A twitch in her fingers, an ache to slap him. Instead, she jerked at her hand, attempting to pull it free, but he held on and so her action had the unintended consequence of bringing her whole body forward, ramming it into his.

She closed her eyes on a husky, terrified groan of surrender.

His nostrils flared. 'They love you, and you have turned your back on them, no matter the consequences.'

'You don't know what you're talking about.'

'Don't I? Unlike you, I have been around to witness the consequences.'

She shook her head, wanting to argue with him, wanting to tell him that they weren't even her family anyway, that if they knew the truth, they wouldn't want her...but how could she begin to explain? Besides, it was a secret she could never tell another soul, for her mother and father's sake. She had to bear this burden herself—she'd learned her lesson after Daniel.

'You think you know my family, but you don't know me, and I have no intention of explaining my innermost thoughts to you. You don't get to know what I'm feeling. That's for me, and me alone. But I will tell you this: if I go home, it will complicate everything. It will potentially overshadow Anton's wedding and ruin my parents' lives. I'm not joking,' she responded, when his lips curled once more into that hateful, derisive half-smile.

'Anton has mentioned your flair for drama,' he said simply, and then she wanted to slap him more than ever. Again she jerked at her wrist, but when he didn't release it, she lifted her foot instead and stamped down on his, satisfied because he was barefoot and she still wore her sandals. She saw his immediate pain response, a tightening in his face, but otherwise he didn't react, and shame at her base instinct quickly followed the satisfaction of having landed another strike against him.

'Screw you,' she said angrily, her breath coming in ragged spurts now as she glared up at him, something else entirely overtaking her. Her gaze dropped to his mouth, and silently she willed him to kiss her.

'You are going home, Amelia. There is no sense arguing about it now.'

'You are insufferable!' she shouted, shocked by her anger, by her lack of decorum, imagining what her tutors would say if they could see her now, wild and overpowered by rage.

'Be that as it may, you shall have to learn to suffer me, for the next week at least.'

'I will swim to shore if you do not turn this boat around.'

He laughed. He actually laughed!

Amelia couldn't take it any more. She lifted her small fists and pummelled his chest, tears of frustration and impotence sparkling on her lashes. 'I hate you!' she said. 'How dare you do this to me? How dare you?'

'This conversation is futile,' he said. 'The next time this boat stops, it will be in a Catarno port. I suggest you take the next week to make your peace with that, and start working out how you can make amends to your long-suffering family.'

Her nostrils flared at his haughty, judgemental tone.

'In the meantime, your bedroom is through there. As

you clearly can't stand being around me,' he said, with indolent mockery layered over the words, 'I suggest you go and make use of it.'

Amelia ground her teeth. He was the most arrogant, infuriating man she'd ever met. 'This is a mistake.'

He lifted one shoulder, careless now. 'Dinner is served at eight. Please feel free to join me. If you think you are capable of behaving with a level of basic civility, that is.'

'You get what you deserve,' she muttered, spinning on her heel and leaving the room, thinking she'd never been so glad to walk out on someone in her life.

CHAPTER THREE

THERE WERE SOME things Benedetto found almost too painful to think about, some memories he kept permanently shelved because they still had the power to tear him down, even now, years after his entire life had been torn asunder.

When he thought of Sasha, he preferred to focus on what their life had been before her diagnosis. Before he'd learned that her fainting and exhaustion and poor eyesight had been caused by an inoperable brain tumour. Before he'd had to come face to face with his greatest fear as a single parent and acknowledge that he would lose her.

His best memories of Sasha were of her as a baby, her sweet, chubby, competent frame dragging across the floor at only five months of age, before she crawled a month later. She'd been walking by eight months, babbling and smiling almost constantly. There'd never been a happier child, he was sure of it.

He remembered her first day at nursery school, how she'd marched in without a backwards glance, confidently making friends and teaching the other children her favourite games, before waving him off with a grin that spread from ear to ear. He remembered how great she'd been at everything she tried—a natural reader, athletic, kind, considerate.

She had been his daughter and so he'd loved her, but it had been impossible *not* to love Sasha. Everyone had felt it. She had been magical.

At her funeral, the priest had said that she'd glowed so brightly, even if just for a short time, and Benedetto had been struck by the truth of that. Perhaps people were born with a certain amount of light to shine, and Sasha had shone all hers out early.

Afterwards, when she was gone, and he'd had to accept that, no matter how much money he'd spent on chasing down state-of-the-art treatments, his failure had equated to her death, he'd been in a state that defied explanation. There were no words to describe his grief. He had been bereft, almost deranged with his sadness.

He'd sought solace in liquor, in women, in dropping out of his life altogether. The fortune he'd been steadily building since seventeen, when he'd founded his first company, had gradually floundered owing to his total inattention.

And Benedetto hadn't cared.

If it hadn't been for Anton stepping in and appointing an interim CEO, it would have all been lost. But Anton had known.

Somehow, he'd understood that the clouds would eventually clear, that Benedetto would come up for air and look for the hallmarks of his life, for some semblance of what had been before, and that there had to be *something* for him to return to. Perhaps Anton had known that the challenge of rebuilding his business would be the one thing to draw Benedetto out of his grief. And so Anton had overseen operations as much as his role as heir to the throne of Catarno had allowed, had made sure that Benedetto would have something to return to one day, even when his personal wealth had been decimated.

Anton hadn't just been there for Benedetto, he'd shown him every step of the way that he would *always* be there for him.

Benedetto owed him an enormous debt of gratitude, and repaying it was immensely important. While kidnapping Amelia, and whatever the hell had happened between them, didn't sit well with him, he knew it didn't really matter. Not as much as helping Anton.

Anton had grown up with the weight of the world on his shoulders, his royal legacy meaning he'd had to be the best at everything, had been scrutinised mercilessly lest he put a foot wrong. It was Amelia who'd had the freedom to enjoy her royal lifestyle without the responsibilities. It was high time she faced up to them, Anton was right.

The first thing Amelia did when she got to her room was drop down onto the bed and scream into one of the pillows, a scream of abject anger and frustration, of a thousand million emotions that were setting her nerves jangling and making her want to dive off the side of the boat.

The second was to move to a window to ascertain the sense of that plan. If she were to jump ship, could she actually swim to shore?

A quick scan of the view from her windows showed her that they'd moved fast—Valencia was just a speck in the distance now. Even for a confident swimmer like her, that would be pushing it.

Or was it that she didn't truly want to escape?

As if to prove to herself that wasn't the case, she went to reach for her camera backpack, to grab her phone, only to remember it had been left in the corridor, presumably when she'd fainted.

With a racing heart—not from fear but from the adrenaline and possibility of running into Benedetto again—she moved quickly, striding across the room, ignoring the pulsing heat between her legs, the yearning that remained unabated in her body, and dragged open the door. She looked left and right, saw no one, so stepped out, looking for her bag.

It was nowhere.

Damn it.

Might it be in the other room? Where he'd taken her when she fainted? She looked down the corridor, decided to chance it, and jogged to that door, pulled it open. A quick inspection showed the room to be empty. But her bag was also missing.

The only conclusion she could draw was that Benedetto had taken it, and, with it, her only way of contacting—

But who would she have called anyway?

Her family? Who'd clearly ordered this kidnapping? They might sympathise with her plight but inwardly they'd be rejoicing at her imminent return, even if it was against her will. And who else was there? The friends she'd unceremoniously dumped when she'd left the country because she wasn't sure if she could trust them either? After Daniel, she hadn't known where to turn. And who could blame her?

Suddenly, Amelia felt so unspeakably alone, so awfully ganged up on, that she ran just as quickly back through the boat, to the solitude of her room. She closed the door and slumped against it, falling to the floor in a heap and dropping her head to her knees, a silent tear trickling down her cheek as she acknowledged the helplessness of her situation.

Going home would be a disaster. She knew it would be.

She knew her family would want to know why she'd left. They'd asked her over and over in email and text, even in the voicemails they'd left when she'd first disappeared. But Amelia hadn't answered. She hadn't been able to.

The discovery of her illegitimacy was still too raw, too painful to discuss, too dangerous to everyone she loved most. Even to her family's position?

That was one of the thoughts that had tortured her most. The civil war was all but a distant memory now, something that had happened three generations back, and yet, for Amelia, the thought of her family being deposed and thrown out by the people had always struck her as particularly horrifying. She'd known even as a young girl she'd do everything she could to avoid that fate.

Unfortunately for Amelia, no matter how well behaved she was, she seemed to find herself getting into some sort of scrape or another. A scandal in high school to do with her friendship group taking drugs—never Amelia, but far be it from her to tell other people how to live their lives— or a cheating scandal at college. Amelia hadn't cheated, but the mud had stuck, and rumours continued to swirl. Even in her own family, she was sure there were suspicions about her grades. The media had loved to print stories about her, so many of them made up, some of them so wild they actually made Amelia laugh, but at the heart of it all was a deep and growing sense of not belonging. Of being different.

And then she'd learned why she'd always felt that way. The root of her sense of displacement.

She *didn't* belong.

She wasn't royal.

The blood of which her family was so proud didn't even flow through her veins.

And in her being she held the power to destroy her parents' marriage, her family's happiness.

Worst of all was the knowledge that the one person she'd turned to when she'd learned the truth, whom she had believed she loved, and had loved her back, had used her secret to blackmail Amelia for financial gain. She'd confided in Daniel because she'd needed to speak to someone about it, and he'd betrayed her. That he still held this piece of information about Amelia, and could use it at any point to damage her and her family, was what had kept her in hiding for two full years.

How could she go back?

How could she risk it?

Fear made her skin crawl.

She stood and began to pace the suite she'd been dumped into, distractedly investigating it simply to assess her situation for the next week. A bathroom, palatial in size and appointment, with a window right on the edge of the boat showcasing yet another spectacular view of the still ever-diminishing Spanish mainland, framed by timber, and placed perfectly behind a claw-foot bath. There was a large shower, a double sink, and when she idly opened one of the drawers she saw that it had been stocked with high-end products—moisturisers, cleansers, even a set of nail polishes, and make-up.

The next drawer housed hair products—a brush, hairdryer, straightener, leave-in conditioner. A quick inspection of the shower confirmed that she'd also been supplied with shampoo, conditioner, toner. A very thoughtful kidnapping indeed, she admitted, but without a hint of a smile, because there was no atonement for what he'd done to her. No atonement for what he *hadn't* done to her either.

Leaving the bathroom, she pressed on the next door along, gasping to discover a full wardrobe of clothes just her size. Her hands ran over the brightly coloured designer outfits—dresses, skirts, bathers, shirts, jackets, everything she could want for a year, not just a week. There were shoes too—sandals and sneakers, as if she might be going to do more than pace a hole in the floorboards of her bedroom!

The final door revealed an office of sorts. It was very small, designed to be tucked out of the way, with a narrow desk pressed to the wall, and cables for a laptop, screen, charger, anything she might need to use while here. But Amelia had brought only her camera and phone, for the simple reason that she hadn't intended to be staying long.

With a sigh, she turned back to the bed and lay down, determined to stare up at the ceiling in the kind of grumpy state a teenager would be proud of, and she spent the next several hours mulling over her predicament and trying to fathom exactly how she could escape this situation.

Because there was no way she could go back to Catarno, and definitely not for Anton's wedding... She simply couldn't risk anything happening that might ruin his happiness. Staying away might have seemed heartless but Amelia had long since decided it was one of the ways in which she was being cruel to be kind.

So how could she get her grumpy captor to understand that?

By eight o'clock, Amelia was famished. She'd been in her room a long time, with no food, no drink, and no desire to go out in search of either. Pride had made her stick to that point. But as he'd 'invited' her to join him for dinner—or rather demanded—she supposed it wouldn't hurt to accede.

She had to work out how to get through to him, after all.

He'd said they had a week together, from which she could only presume he intended for them to travel to Catarno by boat, and that the journey would last that duration. Okay, she could go along with that. A week would definitely afford an opportunity to make him see that she wasn't the person he believed her to be.

Without admitting the truth behind her estrangement, she might be able to convince him of the necessity of her staying away. After all, if he was Anton's best friend, then surely he had a reasonable side.

And pigs might fly, she thought to herself, all hopes of Benedetto being, deep down, a benevolent, kind-hearted billionaire evaporating when she stepped onto the deck to find him glaring out at the ocean as though it had personally committed some great wrong against him.

He was so entrenched in his thoughts that he didn't hear her arrive at first, so she had a moment to study him, and in that moment all of the new-found determination to simply, logically reason her way out of this situation disappeared.

There was nothing reasonable about this man.

Nothing measured or calm.

He was pure animal, pure instinct.

And didn't that just turn her insides to jelly?

She had always regarded herself as a feminist, so it was damned hard to make her peace with this side of her nature. Besides, that would be a job for later. For now, she had to focus on concealing how she felt, what he inspired in her.

First step? Dinner.

Finally becoming aware of her presence, he tilted his

head, even that simple movement imbued with arrogant disdain, so she was aware of her hackles rising, her irritation growing back to the levels it had been earlier. And not just her irritation. Her insides churned and her skin suddenly felt clammy and warm.

She reached up and pulled her hair over one shoulder, seeking the relief of a light ocean breeze against her nape. Instead, her temperature spiked when his eyes fell from her face to her breasts as though they were his and his alone.

And she was back to feeling parched, and totally flummoxed.

'You said dinner would be at eight?' she reminded him crisply, doing her best to tamp down the feelings assaulting her.

But his knowing smile showed that he saw right through her. 'Would you like a drink?'

Amelia moved to the edge of the boat, wrapped her hands around the cool metal balustrade for strength. 'I'll have what you're having.'

'I doubt it.'

'Oh?'

'Whisky?'

Her eyes narrowed. 'Why not?'

He considered her a moment, shrugged as if he had not a care in the world, then disappeared inside. She watched him go, trying not to notice how pleasingly masculine his waist was, how well his trousers moulded his bottom, how tall and athletic he was. She quickly turned back to the water, seeking in it a reprieve, a blast of sanity and calm when everything else was threatening to overwhelm her. But the ocean was at her favourite state—bathed in dusk light, with the moon rising through the orange and pink sky, the waves gentle and undulating, rhythmic and talk-ative, so there was an inherent romance to the water that was definitely no help to her present mindset.

He returned with a whisky, handed it to her, and, de-spite the fact she rarely touched strong liquor, she forced herself to lift it to her lips. It practically burned, yet it also reminded her of her brothers, with whom she'd shared this drink often over the years, and her heart panged with miss-ing them, so she threw back the entire measure to disguise her reaction.

The Scotch acted like a balm on her overwrought nerves and she expelled a long, slow breath before returning the glass to him. Her smile was over-sweet. 'Thank you very much.'

'No problems, Princess,' and she felt things tip beneath her.

It had been a long time since anyone had called her that. Two years, in fact.

'Don't,' she whispered, digging her nails into her palm.

'Why not? You're going home. Isn't it time to get used to your title again? Or would you prefer Your Highness?'

She shook her head in consternation. 'Neither, please.'

'So I shall simply call you Amelia while you are on board?'

'I prefer Millie now,' she corrected.

'Millie is not a princess's name.'

'Maybe not, but it's my name.'

'Are you so angry with your parents that you would even want to disavow your connection to the royal family?'

Her face drained of colour. 'I'd prefer not to discuss it.'

'That's a shame, as we have nothing but time ahead of us.'

'A week,' she said, thinking of how much she had to achieve in six or seven days. Could she change his mind in that time? Could she convince him to let her go? It wasn't long, and yet, with the two of them, it might turn out to be an eternity. Already she felt her nerves stretching well past breaking point.

'Tell me how you know my brother,' she invited, surprised that her voice could emerge so calm when her insides were fluttering.

'We met a long time ago.' His answer was short, his gaze direct, yet he was holding so much back, she couldn't help but laugh.

'That's funny?'

'No, but how assiduously you're trying not to answer my question is.'

It was clear that Benedetto was not a man used to being called out. He glowered for a moment before something like a smile flickered on his face, like lightning way out on the horizon, so quick and breathtakingly bright that you could almost swear you'd imagined it.

'We met through a mutual friend when I was in my twenties. Younger even than you,' he drawled, as if to remind them both of the age gap between them.

She narrowed her eyes. 'Which was how many years ago?'

'Twelve.' He moved closer, lifting a hand to her face on the pretence—and it was most definitely a pretence—of tucking hair behind her ear, to contain it in defiance of the light sea breeze. 'I am thirty-six, Princess.'

Her stomach rolled with the power of these conflicting emotions. Desire warred with frustration, and fear. She wasn't a princess, she wanted to scream, even when she knew she could never proclaim that to another soul.

'Older than Anton,' she murmured.

His eyes flashed with hers. 'And too old for you.'

'And yet you're touching me.'

'Haven't we already covered that?' he responded, but dropped his hand, so she could have kicked herself for even bringing it up. She glanced away, buying time to assume an expression of calm.

'How come I haven't met you?' she pushed, but he didn't answer immediately, instead gesturing to the table across the deck from them. Amelia eyed it, her stomach giving a little growl as she remembered that she'd been starving moments earlier.

'Happenstance,' he said non-committally. 'I've been to Catarno a couple of times. I've met your parents, your brother. You weren't at home.'

She considered that. 'Uni, perhaps.'

'Or with friends.'

She heard the veiled criticism and bristled. She'd gone to a few high-profile parties in her first year at university and from that moment on she'd been dubbed the Playgirl Princess. On the one hand, she'd been pleased to see that the treatment often meted out to young, single male royals was being dispensed to her—because gender shouldn't determine such things. On the other, it had been spectacularly unfair. In reality, Amelia had worked hard at her studies and had been a member of the track and polo teams, competing at a high level for both. If she'd missed seeing Benedetto, it had probably been because she'd had a meet.

There was no point explaining that to him though. It was all too apparent he'd made up his mind about her. It pained

Amelia to imagine how Anton must speak and think of her, for Benedetto to have formed such a particular dislike.

'Why are you so loyal to him?'

He held out a seat for her, their eyes sparking as she moved towards it. She sat, ignoring the way his hands brushed her shoulders as if by accident, and the way her body responded immediately. How was it that a single touch could unsettle her so completely?

'You don't think he deserves it?'

'I didn't say that.'

Benedetto took the seat opposite, his long legs brushing hers beneath the table. Another accident? Her hand shook as she reached for her water glass, glad to take a sip to dilute the whisky flavour in her mouth.

'I'm just curious,' she continued after a moment in which he didn't speak, 'as to why you'd owe him such an allegiance that you'd consider committing a criminal offence.'

'I've done more than consider it,' Benedetto pointed out. 'And I'm more curious as to why you'd be intent on seducing someone who's kidnapped you. You kissed me before you knew, so you can't blame Stockholm syndrome.'

She actually laughed, it was so absurd, but it was a laugh that bordered on the maniacal, hysterical and unhinged, so she dropped her face into her hands and held it a moment.

'I don't know,' was the simple, honest answer. 'It just felt... I just wanted to.'

A frown jerked at his lips.

'You kept pointing out that you have more experience than me, so presumably you've felt that before. I don't like you. I mean, I really, really actively *dis*like you, and yet there's something about you that...'

'Yes?' He growled.

'Makes me want to tear your clothes off.' She blinked away from him, both embarrassed and proud of her frankness.

'And you haven't felt that before.'

She wanted to lie. She certainly didn't want to give him the ego-boost of admitting he was the only man who'd ever had that effect on her, but to what end? His ego was already full to the brim, a little extra wouldn't make a fundamental difference to his behaviour. 'No.'

He arched a brow, silently imploring her to continue, but Amelia was reticent to discuss Daniel.

'You've dated men?' Benedetto pushed.

Amelia bit into her lip. 'Yes.'

'And?'

'And what?'

'You didn't feel a desire for them?'

Amelia hesitated. 'I've dated men, but only one seriously, and it was...' she searched for the right words, her cheeks flushing pink '...slow to warm up.'

Benedetto's eyes met Amelia's and held in a way that caused her whole body to simmer.

Amelia reached for her water, and was sipping it gratefully, when Cassidy strolled towards them. 'Sorry, guys, I burned the first set of prawns and had to make more. But they look delicious. Hope you enjoy.'

The Australian woman was a veritable breath of fresh air after the intensity of Amelia's conversation with Benedetto—not the conversation itself, but the way she felt when they were alone, as if there were an oppressive weight bearing down on her, making it hard to breathe and think and do anything but crave him.

Cassidy placed their meals down—a serving of enormous prawns in a sticky sweet sauce with a large salad. It was exactly the kind of thing Amelia might have ordered in a restaurant, had it been on the menu, and as her gaze drifted from their dinner to the view, the dusky sky quite breathtaking from the colours that burst through it, she thought how perfect and sublime this all would be under very different circumstances. If she'd met Benedetto in a bar, or on the street, instead of like this.

'So if I'd met you some other way, if we weren't connected through Anton, would you have stopped us from... you know...?'

He reached for his cutlery, slicing through one of his prawns. 'I don't deal in hypotheticals.'

'Sure you do. Every time you consider your options for any decision you're planning to make, you consider the hypothetical outcomes. That is just your way of saying you don't want to talk about this.'

A smile was her reward, his appreciation for her quick retort obvious. 'Fine. Let's imagine then that we met randomly, and somehow ended up in a private space, with the chemistry we share.' He kicked back in his seat, his legs brushing hers again, but this time, they stayed where they were, forming a trap around her own legs, so every time she shifted, even a little, she felt him, the static charge of electricity energising her. 'It's likely we would have shared a one-night stand.'

'Only one night?' she prompted, then could have kicked herself. Was she really offended by his reply to a hypothetical scenario that could never be?

He lifted his shoulders. 'Perhaps a few nights.'

'And then what?'

'We'd part ways.'

'That easily, huh?'

'Why not?'

'I just—it seems like a very limiting way to live your life.'

'That's what I like about it.'

She frowned. 'I don't understand.'

'I have no plans to get married, and absolutely no plans to have children. It shifts the parameters of what my relationships are about.' His eyes scanned hers. 'But I am not a subject we need to discuss.'

Her stomach tightened with frustration, but she let it go for now. There was no sense pushing him. Amelia needed time to regroup and form a new strategy, to reconcile what she'd learned about him tonight and how best to use it to her advantage. Lost in thought, she shifted beneath the table, their legs brushed and it was as though an invisible rubber band that had been tightening around them finally snapped.

He jerked his gaze back to her face, his eyes boring into hers, an invisible war being fought, but Amelia couldn't have said who was winning or who was losing, she knew only that she felt as though she were fighting for her survival. Her breath was held, her body stiff, her senses all finely honed on the man opposite.

'You need to understand, Anton is my closest friend,' Benedetto ground out, pushing back his chair, leaving the battlefield altogether. 'Someone who stood by me when no one else would.' He stared at her. 'And you are his sister.'

Anger fizzed inside Amelia. 'I am also my own person. Me.' She stood, jabbing her fingers towards her chest, to indicate the centre of her being. 'I am not just an adjunct to Anton. I'm not a princess. I'm just Millie Moretti and I wish you'd—'

'Don't say it.' He held up a hand, eyes warning her.

'I wish you'd remember who I am,' she finished defiantly. 'Not act as if my only defining characteristic is being related to Anton. But what did you think I was going to say?' she demanded, moving around the table, towards him, until they were toe to toe. 'Did you think I was going to say I wish you'd make love to me?' She threw the gauntlet down between them. 'And if so, why are you so threatened by that?'

'You know why. It can't happen.'

'I don't even know if I want it to happen,' she lied, hating how much she *did* want him. 'But I find it strange that a man with your experience can't be a little more sanguine about the whole affair.'

He responded with a harsh bark of laughter. 'I have kidnapped you and yet you persist in throwing yourself at me. Why?'

If he'd intended to hurt her, then he couldn't have chosen his words more wisely. After Daniel, she'd lost her confidence completely. She'd thought they were in love, but he'd been using her, and it had made her feel dispensable and worthless. She'd sworn she'd never let another man have that kind of power over her again, and yet here she was, not twelve hours after meeting Benedetto, and clearly he already had the ability to wound her.

She shuddered and took a step back, staring at him and trying to make sense of everything, but most of all wanting to escape, to get away from him and his intently watchful gaze.

'You're right.' She shivered despite the fact it was a warm night. 'I must be mad.' There was no other explanation for this. It simply didn't make sense. 'Excuse me.'

She turned on her heel and left. But before she'd reached the door to the corridor, his voice arrested her. 'Wait.'

She stopped walking but didn't turn around. 'What for, Benedetto?'

'I meant what I said before.'

She sucked in a breath.

'If you weren't his sister, and we'd met, as you proposed, in some other way, you would already be naked in my bed. This is not one-sided, Princess.'

She gasped, spinning to find him standing right behind her, so close they were almost touching. 'I don't know what to say to that.'

He held a finger up to her lips, to silence her anyway, but it was an incendiary touch. Sparks ignited.

'Don't say anything. There's no point. It's never going to happen between us so whatever we might be tempted to, it's a far better idea if we just…ignore each other from now on. *Va bene?*'

CHAPTER FOUR

IGNORE HER? YEAH, RIGHT. Given the lack of other occupations, Princess Amelia Moretti had taken to sunbathing on the deck in one of the swimming costumes Cassidy had bought for her, which—Cassidy being a free spirit who'd grown up surfing—was barely sufficient to cover Amelia's body.

His dreams had been filled with Amelia, with imaginings of her, naked and sensual, straddling him so her long hair formed curtains around her face, and yet now that he stared at her in a way that was making it impossible to keep his distance, he realised how much more desirable her body was in the real world, how much more beautiful and graceful, than he'd been able to conjure in his dreams.

So ignoring her wasn't going to work, but nor could he act on his feelings.

Which basically put him in a form of hell for the next six days.

There was one way he could stay true to what he knew to be the right thing.

Eyes on Amelia, he removed his phone from a pocket and loaded up a text to Anton.

I have her. She'll be home within the week.

He sent the message but didn't experience an accompanying sense of relief. If anything, knowing that Anton was aware of the predicament felt strangely oppressive. It also felt like a direct betrayal of Amelia. To whom he owed nothing! And yet he found he couldn't completely disregard her obvious misgivings about returning home.

From Benedetto's perspective, the royal family of Catarno was surprisingly normal and loving, all things considered. He'd never had an example of that, of a real family. He'd been an only child and his father, while not physically abusive, had drunk too much and had a short fuse, meaning it hadn't taken much for him to lose his temper and explode at whomever happened to be nearby—Benedetto, or Benedetto's mother. As children in volatile situations often did, Benedetto had become adept from a young age at appearing to ignore the outbursts, to compartmentalise his fear and panic responses. When his father had died of a heart attack, and Benedetto was only fourteen, he'd been relieved.

Despite the fact the death had plunged Benedetto and his mother from living hand to mouth to abject poverty, the silence and lack of living on tenterhooks had been an immense relief, for both of them. They'd been happy, but only eighteen months later, his mother had been talking on the phone and stepped out from the kerb right into a bus. She'd died instantly. Her, he did mourn.

So his experience with family was limited. Meeting Anton's brother and parents had blown him away—to see the easy love and connection, the way they were all so respectful of one another.

And Amelia had simply turned her back on that, as though it held no value whatsoever. It was a callous, childish, hurtful thing to have done, and yet he wasn't sure Amelia was any of those things.

True, he barely knew her, but his childhood had made him an excellent judge of character. He also didn't have the sort of pride that would prevent him from admitting when he'd made a mistake, and at least on this score he had, potentially, been wrong about Amelia.

And so what? he asked himself angrily. What did it matter to him? Beyond the wedding, he wouldn't need to see her again. She'd be free to live her life.

And what would that look like?

Would she stay in Catarno? Would the wedding be the start of a new phase in her relationship with her parents and siblings? Or would she escape again as soon as she possibly could? Return to Valencia, or somewhere else, now that her cover had been blown?

She turned at that moment, tilting her face. He wasn't sure if he'd moved, or done something else to draw her attention, but her eyes flicked sidewards and landed directly on his—catching him staring at her, pondering. He didn't look away. He held his ground, arms by his sides, every part of him focused on her.

She tilted her face away again, looking out to sea, her expression mutinous.

'It's a far better idea if we just...ignore each other from now on.'

He'd said it. It was his idea, and it was the right idea, so why did he find his legs carrying him across the deck towards her against his own better judgement?

His shadow cast across her chest, long and dark, but it was a warm enough day not to make a hint of difference to Amelia's enjoyment. If anything, his proximity fired something new to life inside her, so she stretched languidly, shifting one leg over the other, crossing them at the ankles, and positioning an arm behind her head, a study in relaxation.

'Are you wearing lotion?'

She was so angry with him, and yet the hitch in his voice pulled at that anger, undoing it a little, making her vulnerable to an awareness of him she was doing her best to fight.

'Is this your idea of ignoring me?'

'I can hardly hand you over to your family with bright red sunburn.'

She bristled at that. 'I'm not an object,' she reminded him coldly. 'No one is handing me to anyone else.'

'I'll take that as a no.'

She ground her teeth together. 'It's none of your business. I'm not your business, regardless of what you and my brother might have discussed.'

'We have not discussed you often, *cara*.'

The term of endearment surprised her, but it surprised him more, going by the look on his face. He seemed to wish to swallow the word right back up again.

'And yet you appear to know a lot about me. Or think that you do.'

'I know what I've perceived, through your absence. Through how that absence has affected your family.'

She could easily believe her family was suffering, but it was nothing compared to the hell they'd be living through if she'd stayed, and they'd learned what kind of mess Amelia had exposed them to.

'I had no interest in hurting them,' she said truthfully.

'And I can't see why any of that matters to you. Friendship with Anton aside, this is a private matter.'

'He asked me to retrieve you, and so I did.'

She jerked to standing, eyes flashing with his, and it was only when she met his gaze that she began to suspect he might have been deliberately goading her. 'Retrieve me?' she repeated with incredulity. 'Seriously? Like a lost pet, or a missing suitcase or something?'

His smile irritated her even as she was captivated by the way it transformed his features.

'Don't laugh at me.'

'I'm not.' He lifted a hand in surrender. 'You're funny, that's all.'

'I'm not meaning to be.'

He lifted his shoulders. 'You still are.'

She expelled a long, calming breath. 'Did you come out here just to ask me about sunscreen?' she asked, determined to shut down their conversation. Maybe he'd been right the night before? Maybe they needed to either ignore each other or at least pretend to, if every one of their conversations led to an argument.

'Yes,' he said, without moving.

'Well, then, you've done your duty. You can go.' She gestured across the deck for him to leave.

He arched a brow.

'You're the one who suggested we ignore each other.'

'Easier said than done,' he drawled.

'God, Benedetto, you're impossible.'

'So I've been told.'

'I'm serious. You're like a whole bundle of mixed messages. Why don't you just decide what you want and let me know?' And with that, she settled back onto the sun lounger and pulled her glasses over her eyes, feigning sleep.

But not for long.

Not five minutes later a splashing sound alerted her to the fact she wasn't alone, and a quick shift of her head showed Benedetto in the pool across the deck. He was swimming through the water, powerful and confident, and although the pool wasn't Olympic length, he had enough space to complete a lap and turn under water, swimming back the other way, where he paused against the coping, his powerful, tanned arms mesmerising, covered in water and delightfully tempting.

She blinked away.

Only, he was right there, half naked, tanned, wet, relaxed, and even when she knew the smartest thing to do was disappear off the deck and away from temptation, she found herself lasting barely ten minutes before she stood and paced to the edge of the pool, an unimpressed scowl on her face.

'Yes?' he asked at the water's edge, standing with legs braced wide apart, blinking up at her through eyes that were rimmed with dark, wet lashes, hair slicked back showing a high brow.

She glared at him. 'Don't you have work to do or something?'

'I've been working,' he replied with a shrug. 'Late last night, and from early this morning. Does it bother you for me to have a break?'

That wasn't what she'd meant. 'It's none of my business,' she muttered, holding up her hands in surrender. 'It just seems like you're going out of your way to aggravate me.'

'By swimming?'

She raised her brows. 'By swimming when I'm right here.' She gestured to the deck.

'There are two of us,' he pointed out. 'You could go somewhere else if my presence bothers you that much. It's a big ship.'

The water was so tempting, and suddenly all Amelia wanted was to dip into it, just for a moment, to cool off. She'd been lying in the sun for hours and she was quite warm all over. But there was no way she'd show even a hint of her thoughts to Benedetto. There'd be time later to swim—for now, she needed to escape.

'Great idea. Thanks for the suggestion,' she said with mocking obedience in her tone. She followed it up by doing an overly exaggerated salute. 'See you later.'

She felt his eyes on her the whole way across the deck.

Inside, she fixed herself a sandwich and took it to her room to eat, brooding as she stared out at the ocean. Once finished, she decided she couldn't pass the rest of her time sulking and staring into space, and there were limited alternatives on board. And so she made her way back to the library, intending to grab a book. But when she strode in, without knocking, it was to find Benedetto there, hair still wet, body mercifully covered now in a T-shirt and fresh, dry shorts.

'Oh!' She startled, and he looked just as surprised. 'I didn't realise you were in here.'

He regarded her for several seconds without moving. 'Well, I am.'

'I see that now.'

'What can I do for you?'

'I came to get a book.' She gestured to the shelves.

'A book?'

'To read,' she babbled, then clamped her lips together. Caught off guard, she was on the back foot, not sounding as assertive or confident as she wanted. 'As I have literally nothing else to do, I presume you won't mind?'

'I don't mind at all,' he said, waving a hand to the wall of titles. 'Take whatever you want.'

'Oh, thank you so much,' she replied, heavy with angry sarcasm. 'What a considerate kidnapper you are. Is there somewhere online I can leave a five-star rating?'

Another smile, which he was quick to smother, but Amelia saw it and her stomach did a strange flopping motion.

'There's a cinema downstairs, you know.'

She glanced over her shoulder. 'A cinema?'

'And a gym. A spa. I was going to show you yesterday, but then you asked me to kiss you…'

'I seem to remember *you* kissing *me*,' she said, though in fact, while his body had come close to hers, it was Amelia who'd sought his lips. She coloured to the roots of her hair.

'We'll have to agree to disagree.'

'You are seriously the worst.'

His eyes bored into hers. 'Do you want to finish the tour?'

'I can probably work it out for myself,' she said after a beat.

'Afraid to be alone with me?'

She ground her teeth together. 'Of course not. Just trying to follow your instructions.'

'Okay.' He didn't move, and her stomach dropped to her toes, the emotion easily identifiable as disappointment. 'Suit yourself.'

Amelia's lips parted but she left the room before she could say something really stupid and beg him to show her.

Unfortunately, when Amelia made her way to the end of the corridor and down the wide stairs, it was to discover a door at the bottom wouldn't open. Had he known?

With a noise of frustration, she turned on her heel, strode back into his office without knocking, hands on hips. 'It's locked.'

Head bent over some documents, Benedetto took a moment before looking at her. She hadn't really given his desk any proper attention, but now she saw it was incredibly ordered, as though he could only function when everything was in its place. There was a laptop, a pile of papers, a leather-bound diary, and, from where she stood, the back of a photo frame. Curiosity had her wanting to move forward to see what kind of picture a man like Benedetto would keep on his desk, but Amelia would die before she'd show that much interest in his life.

'I'll open it, then,' he said simply, standing.

'Why is it locked? We're on a boat.'

'It's a security feature—the door's self-locking. It doubles as a safe room. There's an alternative bridge down there, a backup command system. In case the boat's ever breached.'

She blinked at him, the thought unsettling. 'Is that likely?'

'I'm a very wealthy man. It's not unlikely.'

She shivered.

'You've lived with security precautions all your life. You can't be surprised by that?'

'I just...you're a private citizen.'

'Yes, with a lot of money, which motivates some people to do very bad things. Hence the security features.'

'What else?' she asked curiously, falling into step beside him.

'Planning your escape or your rescue? I should tell you, neither's likely.'

She blinked up at him. 'Do I need to be rescued?'

'I haven't decided yet,' he said, but without humour. 'Maybe I'm the one who should send out an SOS?'

'Oh?'

'I'm starting to think you're trouble with a capital T.'

'You can always let me off at the nearest port.'

'And call the Catarno guard to come collect you? That's not a bad idea.'

She stopped walking, staring at him. 'Benedetto, listen to me—' She inhaled sharply, searching for words. But how could she get through to him? He seemed so determined, without even a hint of doubt about his plan to return her to the family she'd left for their own good.

'I know you're doing this out of loyalty to Anton. I know you think you're doing the right thing, but you're really not. Nothing good can come from making me go back.'

He stopped walking, stared at her for a long time, silence crackling between them.

'Did someone there hurt you, *cara*?'

She flinched. Not because his term of endearment was unwelcome, but because it was entirely too welcome, too comforting. It made her want to cry to think even for a moment that this man might be on her side. He wasn't. Of course he wasn't. He was operating on Anton's behalf, and while she loved her brother, in this matter their wishes were diametrically opposed. But what if Benedetto saw Amelia's perspective? What if he actually went in to bat for her? She couldn't fathom what it would be like to have a defender such as Benedetto.

'Amelia?' he demanded, his expression pinched, as though genuinely worried about what might have happened to her.

She swallowed hard, blinking away. Yes, someone had hurt her. Daniel had destroyed her childish faith in love, he'd taken her trust and trampled it. And worse, he still knew a secret that had the power to destroy Amelia's family. Fear rose in her throat, making it hard to breathe. What a mess it all was.

'I can't go home.' The words were bleak. 'If you have any decency in your heart, any whatsoever, you'll take me at my word and let me go.'

He looked momentarily surprised and then anguished. 'Why does it bother me,' he mused a moment later, 'for you to say I have no decency?'

Her emotions lurched all over the place. 'I don't know.' A whisper. Tears were threatening. She looked away, determined not to show such weakness.

'Do you know why I decided to take you to Catarno by boat?'

She lifted her shoulders. 'Because it was a sure-fire way of getting me out of Valencia?'

'True, but I have a helicopter on board. I could fly you there tomorrow and be done with this.'

Fear made her heart hurt.

'I thought this would be best for you. To have time to get used to the idea, to work through whatever issues you have with your family, to make your peace with the necessity of seeing them again and being at your brother's wedding.

Of being able to put your best foot forward and show your family that you've changed.'

But Amelia hadn't changed. She was still an illegitimate love child, a secret, a shame. And a target for blackmail because she'd opened her big mouth to the wrong person.

'Am I supposed to thank you?' she whispered, anguished.

'No.' He moved closer, putting a hand on her arm solicitously, staring into her eyes with obvious concern. 'Tell me why you ran away.'

'I can't.' Her voice caught. 'I really can't. But believe me when I tell you it was the best thing for everyone. I can't go home, Benedetto. I can't.'

CHAPTER FIVE

DESPITE HER REPUTATION, Amelia was not prone to dramatic fits but as she said, 'I can't' over and over again, she felt herself growing hysterical, frustrated, terrified of the prospect of being home and having to keep this enormous secret, terrified of what Daniel might do or ask if she returned, terrified that Anton's wedding would be ruined because of her.

Amelia could hardly breathe.

Benedetto grabbed her other arm, shaking her a little, so she looked up at him, eyes huge.

'Hey,' he said firmly. 'Stop. Stop.'

She was trembling, she realised, and weak. Without his touch, she wasn't sure she could stay standing.

'Tell me what's going on. Is it just that you're afraid of their reaction? Because I can tell you this: they love you.' His voice was gravelled. 'They want you back, more than anything.'

She shook her head, stomach in knots. 'You don't understand. I can't. I can't.'

And then, perhaps because he saw no other way to silence her, he claimed her mouth with his own, kissing her hard and fast and desperately, absorbing her panic, her anguish, placating her without words or promises to listen and be her champion, but somehow still reassuring her.

Everything inside Amelia shifted. Her hands lifted to his shirt, bunched into it as if holding on for dear life, as if she couldn't possibly survive without him, as if this kiss and he were her lifelines.

It was all so confusing, so wrong, so right. She whimpered into his mouth, lifted one leg, wrapping her heel behind his knee, then higher, aching to be closer to him, so much closer than this. His kiss grew more urgent, more intense, harder, his tongue lashing hers, his mouth pressing her head back against the wall, until he lifted her, carrying Amelia with her legs wrapped around his waist the rest of the way down the stairs to the door that was locked.

He cursed into her mouth, reached over her shoulder and fumbled the buttons on a keypad; the door swung open. Amelia barely noticed. She was utterly captivated by this moment, by him, by what they were sharing, by how her body was reacting and, most importantly, by the way his kiss was wiping everything else from her mind, so she no longer felt as though she were losing to a rising tide of panic, but surfing along a current of desire that was engulfing her in the best possible way.

Through the door, he strode purposefully to a wide arch and stepped through it. She was conscious of only the surface-level details—a sofa, huge, wide, long, beige in colour, which he laid her down on, barely breaking their kiss for even a moment, his hands pushing at the summery dress she'd pulled on over her bathers while she ate lunch, revealing her near-naked body. She had no self-consciousness around nudity, but this was different. Benedetto stripping her bathers was a whole new level and in the back of her mind she knew she should stop this, slow things down, that they both had reasons for not acting on their attraction, but to hell with it. That kind of rational thought felt just outside Amelia's grip.

She was terrified about going home but when Benedetto touched her, nothing else mattered. Didn't she deserve this? Just a little?

'This is crazy.' He seemed to echo her thoughts.

'I know.'

He pushed up onto his elbow, staring down at her, eyes conflicted, lips tense. 'Amelia—'

'Don't stop,' she pleaded, dropping her hands to his sides and pushing up his shirt, revealing his torso, which she lifted up a little to kiss. He groaned, and the power she had over him was a heady, glorious feeling.

'This is complicated.'

'No, it's simple,' she murmured, arching her back. 'I still don't like you, you know. This is just sex, desire, chemistry, whatever. It doesn't mean anything. That's what we both want, isn't it?'

He looked at her as though she'd spoken in a foreign language. 'Your brother—'

'I'm pretty sure neither of us wants to think about Anton right now. But in case you're worried I'm going to tell him about this, don't be. It's not my style to kiss and tell.'

'Nor mine.'

'Then?' she asked, shifting her hips and, this time, removing his shirt fully, throwing it across the room without looking away from Benedetto.

'We'll both regret this.'

She lifted her shoulders. 'Do you want to stop?'

'What do you think?'

She smiled, her heart lifting. 'I think this is out of our control and that's okay.'

He shook his head. 'That's not generally my philosophy.'

And yet, despite that, they were kissing again, lips melded, hands running over each other, naked bodies writhing, moving so one moment she was on top of him and the next him on her until they rolled off the sofa and onto the floor, both laughing at the unexpectedness of that before they kissed once more, and the passion building between them made laughing or speaking entirely impossible.

Benedetto stepped out of his trousers swiftly, removing a slim leather wallet from his pocket and from that wallet a familiar foil square, which Amelia was delighted to see, as she'd been so swept up in the moment she'd almost forgotten contraception.

He stripped naked and sheathed himself and Amelia's mouth grew dry at the sight of his enormous arousal, the size of him alone quite frightening as she imagined taking him inside her. But then he was back on the floor with her, his weight on top of her body, his mouth seeking hers before he moved to her breasts, kissing her as he had the day before, rolling her nipple in his mouth, tasting, tormenting, his hands at her hips shifting lower, between her legs, separating her there, teasing the entry to her sex, promising so much that she was moaning his name over and over, crying out with nonsensical sounds driven by white-hot need and passion. Finally his tip was there, and she was no longer afraid but euphoric and desperate, so she lifted her hips and pulled him in, crying out with relief as he breached her most intimate space and possessed her in a way she'd never known possible.

Hers was a guttural cry of relief, his of restraint, as he

thrust as gently as he could deeper, deeper, until finally his entire length was buried in Amelia and she grew still, eyes wide, staring at him. He ran a hand over her face.

'Okay?'

His concern touched something deep in her chest. She could only nod.

He kissed her then, his tongue moving in time with each shift of his hips, each powerful thrust, the hairs on his chest rough against her over-sensitised nipples, her whole body on fire, pleasure a violent storm now, rather than just a rising current. She felt as though she were being rocked in a thousand directions; as if her body were entirely unfamiliar to her. Every part of her, every nerve ending, every fibre, was exploding, jangling, radiating a whole new frequency. She scraped her nails down his back, crying out as her body began to quiver and tremble as if she were tipping over the edge of a chasm with no ground in sight, only stars and heaven and beautiful sky. She was flying through the stars, the heavens, all celestial, perfect radiant life encapsulated in her as she dug her heels into the base of his spine and held him deep, held him still, as her muscles tensed and spasmed, her body exploding in a powerful, all-consuming release that left Amelia utterly breathless.

She lay, eyes closed, the waves still rolling over her, the tide still lapping at her sides, and then he was moving again, gently at first, letting her get used to the feeling as her insides were still squeezing with release, and then he began to move faster, his mouth seeking first one breast, then the other, his hands roaming her body freely, moving between her legs, stroking her there as he thrust inside her so the pleasures were almost impossible to bear. And she felt the madness returning, threatening to devour her, she felt pleasure filling each pore of her body and threatening to explode it and then she was on the brink of losing herself once more just as he did, so their euphoria was mutual, shared, a total joining of passion and pleasure, of release and relief.

He weaved their fingers together, holding her hands above her as he stilled, and she felt his release, she felt her own body spasm and cried out because it was all so perfect, so desperately, hauntingly right.

'I—don't know what to say,' she murmured after a long time, when their breathing had returned to normal but neither had moved.

'Do we need to say anything?' he asked, and then he did shift, pulling away from her, rolling to his side, propping up on one elbow to study her.

'I guess not,' she agreed, brows knitted together. Her mind though was swirling with thoughts, awakenings, needs, reassurances. Namely, she wanted to know that this wasn't going to be the only time they experienced that. 'I like you more when you make me feel like that,' she said softly, and he laughed, a sound that filled her body with another kind of pleasure.

She smiled, closed her eyes, turned her head and then blinked languidly, scanning the room for the first time. And gasping. She'd been vaguely aware of an enormous piece of wall-size art when they'd entered but had been too caught up in Benedetto to give it another moment's thought. But now she realised it wasn't artwork so much as windows beneath the water giving the most stunning view of the ocean, which was teeming with brightly coloured fish. She scrambled to sit despite the cataclysmic shift that had just taken place inside herself, and saw that the floor also had a large strip of glass, revealing yet another vista. She reached for his arm and gripped it, simply because she almost couldn't believe what she was witnessing.

'It's so beautiful, Benedetto. It's just incredible.'

He was quiet. She spun to face him, smiling, lost in her appreciation for this room, so didn't see the way he was watching her.

'I've never seen anything like it.'

'It's a nice feature,' he agreed belatedly.

'The stone benchtops in the bathrooms are a nice feature,' she contradicted. 'This is mesmerising.'

She pulled her knees to her chest, rested her chin on them. 'I could stay in here for hours, watching the fish swim by. Or us swim by them, whichever it is.'

'Both.'

'Right.' She smiled again, her eyes trained on the water.

'When we stop, it's better. They become curious and swim right up to the boat.'

'Oh, I'd like to see that.'

'I'll arrange it.'

She resisted the urge to ask him to stop them for ever.

For ever wasn't right anyway, but there would be worse places—and worse people—to hide out with for the rest of her days.

'Do you feel better?'

She blinked, something fraying on the edges of her mind before jolting into her fully, reminding her of their conversation Before.

She turned to face him as he reached for a blanket off the edge of the sofa and passed it to her. She took it gratefully, wrapping it around her shoulders, but it wasn't her body that felt exposed so much as her innermost thoughts and worries.

'I feel pleasantly distracted,' she said honestly. 'Can we just keep doing that? Then I won't have time to worry about home.'

'Why are you worried?' He asked the question gently, perhaps concerned that she might devolve into yet another panic attack. Amelia was surprised by how tempted she was to be honest with him. But she'd confided in Daniel, and he'd taken that information and threatened to use it against her. Amelia had learned she had to keep her secrets close to her chest.

'I've been away a long time,' she said eventually, haltingly. 'But nothing's changed. This is going to be a disaster.'

Silence fell between them, heavy and thoughtful. 'You know, I never had a family like yours,' he said, so slowly she felt as though the words were being dragged from him against his will. 'My dad was a mean drunk who seemed to hate me and my mother. He had a raging temper and would lose it often. She was browbeaten by him, and never argued back. After a while, I didn't either.'

'Were you afraid of him?' she asked, leaning back a little, against Benedetto's chest, craving that closeness, but also wanting to comfort him by being near.

'He was not violent,' Benedetto said. 'At least, not physically, but his outbursts certainly had those characteristics. They seemed to erupt from him totally without his control, a temper that was fierce, unjust, unpredictable, and inconsistent. I felt at times that I was living on eggshells, not afraid for myself so much as my mother, who would wither a little whenever he shouted, belittling her with his cruel, awful insults. He would call her dumb, lazy, ugly, a waste of skin. His names for me were worse. Often he told me he wished I'd never been born, that I ruined his life just by existing.'

Amelia sucked in an outraged breath. 'That's a horrible thing to say.'

'Yes.'

'Did your mother leave him?'

'No. She would still be with him today, I'm sure, if he hadn't done us all a favour and died.'

She flinched a little at his words, but she understood them.

'I was so glad, *cara*. I hated the man. He made our lives a misery and yet we were stuck with him. Many times, I contemplated running away, but I was worried for my mother. In the back of my mind there was always a risk he might become physically violent towards her, and at least by being there, I could protect her.'

'Of course you felt that way. What an unfair burden for a young man to carry.'

'When he died, there were mountains of debts in his name. The estate was a mess. I have never known anything quite like the pain of that poverty, and the joy of our freedom. It didn't matter that we often didn't have enough to eat, or spent weeks at a time sleeping in cars. We were free of him.'

'Are you really, though?' Amelia asked, genuinely curious, pressing a hand to his chest. 'I've often wondered about the wounds left by a childhood like that. The insults spoken by someone who's supposed to love you and instead treats you as though you're worthless. Is there a part of you that still carries those wounds, Benedetto?'

'I'm not stupid enough to deny that,' he said with a lift of his shoulders. 'We are all shaped by experiences, and for the first fourteen years of my life, I lived with a man who told me every day that I was worthless. But if he shaped me,' Benedetto added, fixing her with a steady, cold gaze, 'it was probably for the better. Every day I knew that I would never become like him. I would never allow my temper to get the better of me. I would control my emotions, not the other way around. I would be better than alcohol, gambling, addiction, cruelty. I would prove him wrong. And I did.'

'Yes, you did.'

'When I first met your family, I could not believe how loving everyone was. Your parents seem to enjoy each other's company. They listen to one another's opinions. They are the definition of a team. Your brothers are friends. It's all so amiable and…nice. So warm. I cannot imagine what it must have been like, growing up in that environment.'

She stiffened, the mention of her family something she didn't welcome, bringing their conversation to a place she refused to go.

'To you, from the outside, I'm sure it did seem like that.'

'Does that mean I've missed something? Is it your family you are afraid of?'

'I can't talk about it.'

'Why not?'

'Because I can't.' She pulled up to standing, frustrated, aware of him watching her as she paced to the window. 'My family are fine. Loving, as you say. Almost to a fault. Whatever issues I have with them, and, like anyone, things they do annoy me sometimes and I'm sure that's mutual, I still love them. I don't want to hurt them. But I can't…' Her voice faded off into nothing as she ground her teeth.

'It doesn't matter.' She turned to face him. 'Nothing I say will change your mind, will it?'

He looked at her long and hard, spectacularly naked, strong, handsome, desirable, so close to being perfect that she realised, belatedly, that was exactly the case: Benedetto was a mirage. Stranded with him, she saw only what she wanted to see, but, ultimately, he was going to hurt her, just as Daniel had. She had to accept that.

'I'm sorry. I gave Anton my word.' He rose then, coming to stand in front of her, pressing a finger beneath her chin and lifting it. 'But I also think it is the right thing for you.'

Her smile was laced with sorrow. 'That's just something you're telling yourself to assuage your guilt.'

'They love you. Whatever you're running from, they want to help you. Let them.'

She closed her eyes, the first step in blanking him from her mind, body, and heart. When they'd made love, she'd had some kind of hope that she could get through to him, that maybe he'd come to see things from her perspective, but now she realised: he never would. Sleeping with him was the best she'd ever felt but it was also a mistake, one she couldn't repeat no matter how much she wanted to.

'I'm not an idiot, Benedetto. When I ran away from home, I did so knowing how it would hurt them, knowing what it would mean for all of us. I did it anyway. I weighed up all my options and chose the one that was right—not just for me, but for them too. In fact, it was agony for me, but it had to be done. I did them the courtesy of keeping my reasoning to myself, but that doesn't invalidate it. You're infantilising me and treating me with a complete lack of respect by making me go home.' She pressed a hand to his chest, pushed it lightly, then stepped backwards. 'I'm sorry,

I can't say anything to ease your conscience. You're doing the wrong thing, and you should feel bad about it.'

She was beautiful and softly spoken, the total opposite to how his father had been, and yet her words, so gently delivered, cut him to the quick more than almost anything had in his life. She'd called him out on what he was doing, echoing his own deepest-held misgivings, which he'd pushed aside purely out of loyalty to his friend, but hearing her charges, after what had just happened, put him in a position he couldn't defend.

'I do.'

Her eyes widened, her lips parted. 'But it's not too late. We're only a couple of days out of Valencia. Surely you could fly me back? Take me anywhere,' she pleaded. 'Just not there.'

'I've already told Anton you're on the way.'

She recoiled as though he'd slapped her. 'What?'

'It's done.'

'It's not done,' she whispered, but tears filled her eyes and his gut rolled. He hated himself then, and the promise he'd made Anton.

'But I believe that facing your family and at least explaining to them—'

'You don't know what you're talking about.' She wrapped her arms around her torso, shivering, her beautiful face radiating tension now. 'Imagine if your father was still alive and someone was taking you to him, telling you that it's always better to face your demons, to forgive and forget, would you?'

Despite the fact it was a hypothetical and he'd said he didn't deal in them, he blanched at the very idea.

'See?' she asked with a hollow laugh. 'Isn't that just the slightest bit hypocritical?'

'My father was a monster. Your family is not.'

'No, they're not monsters. They're wonderful, beautiful, loving, selfless people.' She stared at him for several long seconds so he thought she might be about to reveal something to explain why the hell she'd run away, what had motivated all of this. But instead, she shook her head slowly, looked at him as if he'd just slaughtered a cat in front of her, and left without another word.

CHAPTER SIX

FOR TWO DAYS, she ignored him. Two long days and nights. Every now and again he'd catch a glimpse of her, moving through the boat, going to get a book, or watch a movie, or to swim, but she never looked in his direction, even though she must have known he was there. It was as though she was going out of her way to avoid the briefest eye contact. She ate in her room—an unnecessary precaution because, having realised she wanted to avoid him, he would have given her the space necessary to do just that regardless.

After they'd slept together, he'd returned to his office to see a message from Anton on the screen.

You have no idea how relieved we are. I knew I could trust you with this.

The words had hit him in the chest like a grenade.

He'd agreed to help his friend without a moment's hesitation. Of course he had. Having heard only one side of the story, and never having met Amelia, he hadn't given her a second thought. His mind had filled out the facts necessary to make his peace with the whole concept and he'd set things in motion.

But she was under his skin now, a living, breathing, feeling human who had made it perfectly clear over and over again that she didn't want to return to her family.

He didn't agree with that choice. Regardless of Anton's request, he still believed it was better to face things head-on, particularly with people you loved. Knowing how he'd loved Sasha, understanding that there was nothing he wouldn't do for her, he recognised the pain Amelia's parents were feeling. He'd wanted to help.

But what authority did he have to control Amelia's life? She was right.

He didn't know anything about her circumstances. He had no idea what had motivated her to leave in the first instance. Forcing her home might make things ten times worse.

And if it did? Was it enough to be with her? Could he stand by her side as she faced whatever it was she feared? Could he offer her that at least? Was it a way of assuaging his conscience, just as she'd accused him of? And would she accept?

With a sense of determination that spurred him to take a step he'd never thought possible, he reached across his desk, picked up the photograph and moved through the ship, in search of Amelia and, he hoped, some form of redemption.

'Do you have a moment?'

Amelia startled, the sound of being spoken to directly after days of silence making her jump out of her skin.

The sight of Benedetto, whom she'd been forcing herself to avoid so much as looking in the direction of, made her skin flush and her heart race as a whole host of memories slammed into her. She blinked away quickly, staring instead at the dusk-lit ocean.

'There's something I want to explain to you.'

It was childish, but she still didn't speak. Partly because she didn't trust herself to. Her voice was hoarse from disuse anyway, but emotions were also crowding in around her.

She stood her ground though, jaw set mutinously, eyes focused ahead, and he remained standing at her side for several long seconds, then expelled a sigh, placing something down beside her. Despite herself, Amelia's eyes shifted, and she recognised the photograph from his desk, though she'd seen only the back.

Now that it was pointed towards her, she saw a smiling little girl looking back at her with dimples in her cheeks and eyes that seemed to sparkle with life and vivacity, so Amelia couldn't help smiling back. This child was, she suspected, the kind of girl who had that effect on everyone, even when rendered as a two-dimensional image.

'That's Sasha. Sash.' He cleared his throat. 'My daughter.'

She startled, jerking her gaze to his face. 'You have a daughter.'

'She died. Six years ago. After eighteen months of illness, treatments, the longest, slowest goodbye, and in the end, she was in so much pain that it was almost a relief when she—for her sake—but I was destroyed by it, Amelia.'

Amelia's eyes filled with tears and every shred of anger and rage and rightful indignation dropped away completely.

She stood up, wringing her hands in front of her.

'I'm not telling you for sympathy,' he responded gruffly, forestalling any effort she might make on that score, as if it would have been unwelcome anyway. 'I'm telling you because you need to understand. When she got sick, helping her became my sole focus. I pushed everyone away. I neglected my business. Lost most of my money, assets; it didn't matter. All I cared about was Sasha, and finding the right doctor, the best doctor, the treatment that would prove to be the miracle we needed.'

Silence surrounded them; the air pulsed with emotion.

Amelia stared at him, lost for words, full of feelings.

'And everyone left me.'

Her heart shattered.

'No one wanted to be near me; they didn't know what to say, what to do.' His voice was gruff, factual. Slow to form, the words dredged from the depths of his soul. 'Except your brother. Anton visited. Brought Sash toys. Came to stay with me at the end. Comforted me when she left. And afterwards, when I would have drunk myself into an early grave, he was the one who kept me tethered—just enough—to this world to fight back when I was ready. He was the hand reaching out for me, pulling me some of the way out of the worst grief I can describe, guiding me back to myself, my business. I owe him…everything.'

Pride and love for her older brother filled Amelia's heart, but there was also such hurt for Benedetto. She moved closer, picked up the photograph, looked at it. 'She has the most beautiful smile.'

'Yes.'

Benedetto's jaw was clenched, as though he was grinding his teeth, trying to control his emotions.

'So when he asked you for help, you agreed without hesitation.'

'I said I'd bring you home, whatever it took. I couldn't fail him. I can't.'

Amelia nodded slowly, wistfully, replacing the photo on

the tabletop before pressing a hand lightly to Benedetto's chest.

'I had no idea—' his voice was gruff '—when I agreed to help, that it would cause you so much pain. You're nothing like what I thought you'd be.'

'Spoiled, selfish, thoughtless?' she prompted, because he'd made his assumptions abundantly clear.

'Maybe I wanted to think that, to make it easier to go through with this.'

'You're still going through with it though,' she said, gesturing to the ocean that surrounded them. 'Because of what you feel you owe Anton.'

He closed his eyes a moment. 'I want to help you too.'

'Oh?'

'I don't know what happened in Catarno to cause you to leave. You clearly don't want to tell me, and that's fine. I don't know what you're running from, but, if it helps, I can be there with you, when we arrive. I'll stand with you as you face your family. Whatever will make this easier, I'll do. I owe you that much, at least.'

A great big ball of feeling exploded in Amelia's chest. Sadness, relief, happiness, something else she couldn't identify—affection and gratitude and something shimmery that made her whole body feel as though it were tingling.

'Excuse me, Millie?' She was jolted from the wonder of those feelings by Cassidy's voice, from just a small distance away. 'Will you be eating in your room or do you want to sit out here? It's a gorgeous night.'

Amelia blinked, slow to compute.

Benedetto reached out, laced their fingers together. 'Have dinner with me.' But even as he said it, she felt the doubts in his voice, the hesitation, the unwillingness to surrender. Their attraction was something they hadn't fore-shadowed, and it complicated everything, but that was worse for him.

Having heard what Anton meant to him, and why, she could well imagine Benedetto not wanting to sabotage their friendship by getting in a relationship with Anton's younger sister. And yet here he was, holding her hand, asking her to trust him.

Her heart stretched and thumped.

How could she?

How could she ever trust anyone again?

But this was just a meal. Dinner. It wasn't a lifetime commitment. And she didn't have to bare her soul to him just because he'd shared something so personal with her. Confident she could control this, Amelia turned to Cassidy. 'I'll eat out here.'

The ocean created the backdrop audio, a gentle lapping against the sides of the boat, rhythmic and seductive, sooth-ing. When they were alone again, Benedetto gestured to the leather lounge that was at the top of the infinity pool, which was lit with stunning underwater lights, giving it a magical appearance.

Amelia allowed him to guide her to the seat, to pull her down beside him to rest back against him and listen to—and feel—the steady thrum of his heart, the intake of his breath, the good, solid, dependable movements of his body, his offer so exactly what she'd wanted from almost the first moment she'd met him.

'So you want to be my executioner and saviour,' she murmured, tracing invisible patterns on his knee.

'No one is going to want to execute you,' he said gruffly, pausing for a moment, and Amelia was quiet, waiting.

'When Sash was younger, before she got sick, she wanted to take a day off school. I can't remember why. She was fighting with a friend over something silly. She was only seven or eight.'

Amelia was still, listening, glad that he was speaking to her about his daughter, glad to hear about the beautiful child whose life had been extinguished far too young.

'Eight,' he said, snapping his fingers. 'Because her teacher was Mrs Fauci. I let her stay home. She had a nanny, a nice old lady who loved her like a grandmother, and I thought that was appropriate—the least I could do, really, as she had no one else to fill that role.'

'What about her mother?' Amelia asked softly. 'And her mother's family?'

'Her mother, Monique, was a woman I'd known for about three nights, when I was nineteen. She didn't tell me she was pregnant. The first I knew about Sash was when they turned up on my doorstep, Monique handing the baby to me telling me she didn't want anything to do with her.'

Amelia's stomach twisted.

'I didn't want a kid,' he said on a gruff laugh. 'Hell, my business was taking off, I felt like I was king of the world. And suddenly, I had to get a nursery ready, hire a nanny, work out how to fit a child into my life. And what if I turned out to be like him?' His voice sobered. Amelia turned a little, so she could see Benedetto better, rearranging herself so that instead of leaning back against him she was facing him, legs over his. He turned to look at her, a haunted expression in his eyes. 'It was my greatest fear. How could I know, until I had her in my life, that I wouldn't be just like my father? That I wouldn't lose it at the slightest provocation? That I wouldn't say things to her I couldn't take back?'

'You're not like him.'

'No, I'm not,' he agreed. 'You don't know how relieved I am to be able to say that. I raised my voice at Sasha only once in her entire life, and it was when she was two years old and was reaching for a pan that was filled with boiling water. She couldn't see above the stove, but if she'd got hold of it, if it had fallen on her—'

'That's a perfectly reasonable reaction,' Amelia responded.

'She turned to look at me with such surprise, and then giggled and ran into my arms. She was all that was good in this world.'

'She sounds amazing.'

He didn't reply at first, simply stared out at the ocean, one hand on Amelia's thigh. It was a balmy night, the kind Amelia loved. She'd always adored the heat, preferring it when she could sleep in just her underwear with a light sheet.

'So when she was eight, she stayed home from school,' he said, disorienting Amelia with his segue back to a conversation she'd forgotten about. 'Her nanny—Mary—told me later that they'd played Uno all day, Sasha had eaten well. She was happy that night when I tucked her into bed. But the next morning, she didn't want to go to school again. I insisted she go, she refused. It was rare for her to dig in her heels. Sasha was always happy and obliging and easygoing, so for her to get so worked up, I didn't know what to do. I let her stay home again. Mary told me they had another great day together. I don't know who enjoyed it more, honestly.'

Amelia smiled softly, pulling her hair over one shoulder as a gentle breeze rustled past them.

'The same thing, the next day. She just wouldn't go back. She wouldn't tell me why.' His eyes flicked to Amelia's. 'After a full week of this, we had a normal weekend, and then Monday morning came around. I was determined to get her to school. Again, she refused. I had no idea what was going on, so finally I called her teacher to see if there was something more at play.'

'And?'

'Nothing significant,' he said, lifting one hand palm up into the air. 'But then she explained how staying away from school can make even the smallest things seem like a huge deal. That our minds can build it up to be a bigger problem, that the longer we stay away, the harder it gets to go back. Mrs Fauci said the only solution was to bring her to school, even if she was in floods of tears. That within an hour she'd be over it.' He turned to look at Amelia, eyes scanning her face. 'She was right. On the Tuesday morning, I drove her to school myself, walked her to class. She was furious with me, glared at me, refused to give me a hug— completely unlike her—and I spent all day worrying that I was the worst parent in the world, that she would hate me for ever. She came home, smiling, with a story she'd written on bright green paper, and a card all her friends had made because they'd missed her so much.'

Amelia smiled, and her heart hurt too. 'You're a great dad.' She didn't know why, but she used the present tense, perhaps because she figured it wasn't a position you could lose. Even though Sasha had passed away, he was still her father and always would be.

'I got good advice from Mrs Fauci,' he replied. 'And was quaking in my boots going through with it.'

Amelia laughed. *'You?'*

'Oh, *si*, absolutely. It was so unusual for Sasha to be angry with me, I was sure I was messing everything up monumentally.' He squeezed Amelia's thigh. Across the deck, there was movement—Cassidy was setting the table.

'I don't know why you left Catarno, but I wonder if the longer you stay away, the harder it's going to be to go back.'

She bit into her lip, surprised at how the comparison didn't reassure her. 'It's different.'

'Sure, the circumstances are, but what about the psychology? You've been gone over two years. Isn't that a part of it?'

On some level, he was probably right, but it wasn't so simple. 'I never planned to go back.'

'Never?'

I couldn't. She was so tempted to tell him the truth, but it was too awful, too shameful. Not just the truth of her parentage, but her idiocy in having shared her discovery with Daniel, putting herself in a position to be blackmailed. She couldn't allow history to repeat itself. She gulped, physically quashing that temptation, knowing she needed to take control of what was happening between them.

'I think we should talk about this,' she said, biting into her lower lip.

'This?'

'Us.'

She felt him stiffen and it was all the confirmation she needed that the conversation was imperative.

'You told me you don't do relationships.'

'*Si.*'

'Well, I'm definitely not looking for a relationship either.' As soon as she said it, she felt the world tilt. It was so important to cling to that, to remind herself of what had happened with Daniel and why she'd been so careful ever since. 'I don't want this to get out of hand.'

'It won't.'

Her smile was wistful. 'You sound so confident.'

'Believe me, *cara*, as incredible as I find you, I will have no problems walking away from you after the wedding.'

She shivered inwardly. 'Because you don't do relationships?'

'Correct.'

'How come?'

'I could ask you the same thing.'

Amelia inhaled quickly. 'I…' She hesitated, aware that she was getting dangerously close to confiding in him. But surely she could offer a partial explanation, nothing to do with her mother's affair, but just a little insight into what had happened with Daniel? 'I suppose I learned my lesson,' she said haltingly. His eyes probed her face as he waited for more. Amelia sought the right words. 'I was dating a guy. I really cared for him; I thought we were in love,' she said with a lift of one shoulder, tilting her face to study the moon as it brightened in the sky. 'But he was just using me.'

'Why do you say that?' His question was calm and measured, as though drawing the information from her to assess its validity.

'It became apparent, when we broke up. He—' she broke off a moment, '—betrayed my trust, in the worst possible way. It made me doubt everything I knew about everyone. If I could be wrong about Daniel, who was I right about? I thought I knew him,' she said, shaking her head. 'I was an idiot.'

'No,' Benedetto contradicted. 'You just trusted the wrong person.'

She grimaced. He made it sound so simple, but it was a mistake that she would have to live with for the rest of her life. She'd never stop worrying about what she'd told Daniel. The power she'd given him to hurt her, and her family, would never go away.

'I won't make that mistake again,' she muttered.

'So it's easier to trust no one?'

She turned to face him, eyes unknowingly blanked of emotion, and nodded slowly. 'It's easier not to rely on anyone,' she amended. 'Whatever this is—' she gestured from her chest to his '—I want us both to be clear: it doesn't mean anything. It's not real, and neither of us owes the other anything. Okay?'

CHAPTER SEVEN

IT WAS A relief to hear her say that. The moment Amelia put boundaries around this thing, Benedetto recognised that a part of his misgivings had come from an anxiety around hurting her, leading her on.

'I'm glad to hear you say that,' he said, honestly. 'I didn't want to give you the wrong idea.'

A smile tilted her lips. 'That you're madly in love with me? Don't worry, you haven't.'

It was easy to return her smile, but he knew he owed her more of an explanation. 'It's not you. It's who I am.'

'I know that,' she said quietly.

'After Sash—even before Sash,' he corrected. 'I hated the idea of being in a relationship.'

'I guess your parents weren't the best example.'

'True.'

'So you've avoided commitments all your life?'

'Until Sasha,' he said, stroking his chin.

'Well, I'm not looking for commitment,' she said. 'As soon as I can, I intend to disappear from everyone all over again.'

'You can't do that.' He thought of Anton's family, of how much they loved Amelia, of how painful it was to lose a child, and hated the thought of her leaving them for a second time.

But Amelia only offered a wistful half-smile in response.

'So beyond this boat trip, we can forget we ever knew each other.'

Was that relief Benedetto felt again? She was making this so easy for him.

'But while we're here?' he prompted, watching her carefully, so he saw the way a delicate pulse point at the base of her throat sped up.

'While we're here,' she murmured, 'I think we should enjoy the ride.' She pulled her hair over one shoulder. 'It doesn't mean anything, Ben, but that's not to say we can't have fun…'

She moved a hand to his chest, pressed it there, her body sparking at the simple, innocuous touch. Their eyes met. She felt something stir inside her. Despite what she'd just said, and the important clarification she'd needed to make to protect herself and Ben from any possible complications, there was something about being so close to him, after their conversation about Sasha, that felt so intimate, as though she had a hotline to parts of his soul that were fundamental and raw. She moved closer instinctively, her lips almost meeting his.

'I like being friends, rather than fighting.'

'Fighting was fun too,' he said with a grin, but then he was kissing her quickly, as though magnetically drawn to her, and Amelia was moving too, urgently, needing him with all of herself, her body flooded with desire and pleasure and a thousand things she couldn't define and didn't recognise. He moved first, lifting her easily, carrying her against his chest, carrying her away from the deck, into the corridor and towards her bedroom.

Inside, they fell to the mattress together, and Amelia rolled over, straddling him, running her hands over his torso as he gripped the edges of her dress and lifted it, groaning when it came over her head, revealing her naked breasts. His hands roamed her body, cupping her, pulling at her nipples as she moved over his arousal, her underwear and his clothes unwelcome barriers to the coming together they both desperately needed, but even through the fabric she could feel his hardness and she rolled her hips, moaning at how close she was to feeling him, at how perfect it was to be this close. Torture and pleasure, all wrapped up inside her.

'God, Benedetto, this is so—I didn't know—'

He kissed the words back into her mouth, as if he'd said them himself or thought them. She arched her back and he moved to sit, his mouth finding her nipples, then seeking her lips once more, his kiss moving over her collarbone, his stubble dragging against the sensitive flesh. His hands cupped her bottom, moving her over his length, holding her down, lifting her up, separating her buttocks, inviting her, needing her, wanting her until finally he made a guttural noise and rolled her onto her back, stared down at her with breath hissing between his teeth.

'What is it?' She brushed her hair out of her face. 'Is something wrong?'

'You could say that.'

Amelia's heart thumped.

'I don't have protection. Tomorrow I'm stocking every damned room in this boat. But for now—wait here.'

'Oh.' Relief flooded her; she smiled. 'Okay.'

He was back almost immediately. 'You ran?' she teased, biting into her lip, his need for her the hottest aphrodisiac she'd known.

'A professional sprinter would have eaten my dust,' he agreed, pushing out of his trousers and rolling a condom over his length before coming back over her, kissing her, moving a hand between her legs, separating her thighs, bringing himself to her sex, pausing there a moment before entering her in one single motion, hard, fast, desperate, a thousand times more filled with need than the last time they'd done this when it had been new and different and they'd been exploring their attraction.

They'd agreed to the terms of this, and Amelia was glad, because it meant she could revel in the physical side of their attraction without worrying that it would get out of hand. They were just sleeping together. It didn't mean anything. It was simple, sensual, perfect...

But when the sun dawned the next morning, Amelia couldn't totally ignore the maelstrom of her feelings, so she was grateful that when she woke, Benedetto was no longer in her room. In another time and place, she would have wanted to roll over and lean into the nook of his arm, to rest her head on his chest, to kiss him awake. But that wasn't what they were.

This wasn't a real relationship, and he was the last man on earth she could trust. After Daniel, she'd been wary. Daniel had been a wolf in sheep's clothing.

At least with Benedetto, he'd been a wolf all along. She'd

known from almost the first moment they met that he was her enemy, so at least there was no risk of a shock betrayal.

Nothing could change the fact that he was taking her home, even when he'd explained his relationship with Anton and why it had mattered to him so much to do whatever Anton asked of him. She was so angry with Benedetto, even when she forgave him completely, and none of it made any sense.

She could never accept his decision.

She'd thought she might be able to change Benedetto's mind in the course of the trip to Catarno, without disclosing the truth behind her disappearance, but, understanding what she did now, she knew that she'd never succeed. And weirdly, she wasn't sure she could even ask it of him. It shifted something inside her to recognise that she cared more for Benedetto's obligations to Anton than she did almost anything else. Why did that bother her so much?

Why did she feel such a deep sense of unease to recognise that there were few things that she cared about more than Benedetto's sense of duty? Was it because of how much he'd lost? Did she feel so sad for him that she was willing to sacrifice herself?

Of course not.

If she could escape, she would, even now, because her family deserved that. True, there would be a scandal attached to her no-show at the wedding, but it would be short-lived, and the royal family's PR machine would swing into action, coming up with some reason or other to explain it all away.

It would be better than the risks her return would bring. Unfortunately for Amelia, the chance of escape wasn't likely to occur, so she had to resign herself to her fate—in a matter of days, she'd be home.

'What is that?' Amelia asked from her vantage point on the deck, eyes focused on the land that was so close the beach umbrellas were visible.

Benedetto finished his strong black coffee before replacing the cup on the table between them. 'Crete.' The Greek island was not far from Catarno. It was almost time.

He turned to her, scanned her face. 'Have you ever been?'

'As a teenager,' she said with a smile of reminiscence. 'We used to sail the Med in the summer.'

The important thing was to get Amelia back to her family. It was his mission; he'd promised Anton. But the closer they got, the more inevitable their parting—and return to reality—became, he found himself wanting to stall. Just a little. 'Would you like to stop?'

She blinked across at him. 'Stop?'

Just a small delay. It wouldn't hurt… 'For lunch. You can get your land legs before we arrive in Catarno.' He contemplated that a little longer. 'We could stay here overnight.'

The second he'd said it, he realised how stupid the offer was. Where would they stay? A hotel? What were the chances her identity wouldn't be leaked by someone? Besides, wasn't there a risk she might run away again?

As soon as the idea occurred to him, he dismissed it.

She didn't want to go home, but, somehow, he was sure she understood why it was important to face her family. To be there at Anton's wedding. She wasn't a coward; he knew that much was true.

'Stay overnight, on the island?'

'Or the boat, but in port. For privacy reasons,' he said, relaxing into the idea of this. 'What do you think?'

What did she think? Amelia stared at him, her heart hammering, words hard to form. Was it possible he was trying to extend their time together? That he knew they were only a day away from Catarno, at most, and wanted to eke out their remaining time as long as possible?

But only yesterday, Amelia had promised herself that if she had a chance to escape, she would take it. Wasn't that exactly what was being presented to her?

Amelia chewed on her lower lip, totally lost, her heart stretching and twisting painfully in her chest, because she knew what she had to do but she couldn't make herself happy about it.

'Okay,' she agreed, forcing an over-bright smile to her face. 'Just give me a minute to get ready.' She walked towards the door that led to her rooms. 'Oh.' She snapped her fingers as if just thinking of it. 'Where's my camera backpack? I'll bring it in case there are some photos I want to take.'

'I'll get it,' he said without hesitation, which made her feel a thousand times worse, because the backpack also had her phone, and she knew she would need both in order to get off Crete.

'Thanks. I won't be long.'

They took the smaller speedboat into shore, Benedetto at the helm, looking every inch the devilishly handsome billionaire as the wind swept his dark hair from his brow and the water dappled across his shirt. Sun streamed across their path, warming them even as the breeze served to temper the heat of the day.

Amelia's heart was in her throat the whole way. She noticed a thousand tiny details about Benedetto, as if her unconscious mind was trying to commit him to memory, as if she needed to cement him into her soul before leaving.

Leaving.

Was she really going to do this?

Wasn't it her obligation?

Nothing had fundamentally changed since he'd scooped Amelia out of her life and brought her back here. She was still an illegitimate, secret daughter, the product of an extramarital affair that had the potential to destroy her family and undermine her parents' place on the throne. She was still a guilty secret. And Daniel was still out there with this knowledge, ready to blackmail her again.

Nausea rose in her throat and she blinked it away, gripping the strap of her backpack more tightly.

The ocean changed colour around them, going from a darker shade of blue to a turquoise so clear it was almost transparent, and gradually they were surrounded by other watercraft—boats, jet skis, holiday pleasure-seekers enjoying the sunshine and salt water.

Benedetto expertly steered them away, towards the marina, pulling them into a dock there and cutting the engine. His smile when he turned to her was completely without suspicion.

Her stomach squeezed painfully and before she could control her unconscious mind, she indulged a secret fantasy of pretending this was real. That they were two different people, with different pasts, who were willing to give this thing a real go, and see where it went…but it was an impossible dream.

'Ready?'

Her stomach dropped but she nodded. 'Let's go.'

A deckhand appeared from the marina to tether the boat, and once they were secured, Benedetto hopped out first then held out a hand for Amelia. She put hers in it, ignoring the spark that travelled the length of her arm, forcing a smile to her face. 'Where to first?'

They walked the ancient streets of the city, through narrow, winding cobbled paths with brightly coloured buildings on either side. Window boxes filled with geraniums and rosemary burst with brightness and fragrance, potted citrus plants decorated doorways, children played happily around them, and as they crossed the square, a group of old men in vests and caps began to sing happily, spontaneously, bowls of seafood in their laps, a card table set up with food and a rounded bottle of wine.

Amelia's chest hurt. This was so like her country, her culture, her people, that she felt such a wave of homesickness it almost paralysed her. She stopped walking, looked around, her breathing growing raspy.

'Amelia?'

'It's just…so familiar,' she said wistfully. 'It reminds me a lot of home.'

He reached out and squeezed her hand. 'You'll be back soon.'

He'd completely mistaken her feelings. Or perhaps he hadn't. She was homesick, she did want to go back, in a way. But missing home wasn't the same as being able to return. She was exiled.

Self-imposed, but no less binding.

They stepped into a very old church on the edge of the square, admiring the architecture, the pillars, but always in the back of Amelia's mind was the knowledge that this would be the end. That this was when she'd escape. She *had* to escape. Didn't she?

But what if she didn't? What if she stayed with him? What if she agreed to let Benedetto support her—not in talking to her parents about the reason she'd left, but just by being her strength. By helping her get through it. What if he just acted as her friend, nothing more, nothing that would cause issues for him and Anton?

'You're distracted,' he murmured, brushing a hand over her hair.

Her heart slammed into her ribs and out of nowhere, she imagined them in a church filled with loved ones, his touch like this a deeper promise and pledge. Her heart trembled.

'Am I?'

'Hungry?' he prompted, still with no idea how deeply she was considering her next move.

'Yes,' she lied, for her stomach was far too knotty for food.

'I know a good place. Come on.'

She might have expected a fancy restaurant but instead he'd chosen an out-of-the-way seafood café with seating for about twelve people and views over the water. It was intimate, and the privacy of their booth meant she had no concerns about being spotted, so removed her hat and glasses.

They ordered something light, and some drinks, and Amelia imitated a relaxed pose, leaning against the leather banquette, looking out to sea. Their drinks came first, and while they waited for their food, Benedetto made easy small talk, telling Amelia about a project he was working on in mainland Greece, a package of three high-rises.

She listened, genuinely fascinated by his work, his world, his success. Their food arrived and they continued to talk, but in the back of her mind Amelia was angsting over everything. She couldn't decide what to do, but, ultimately, self-preservation had to win out.

When their plates were cleared and coffee ordered, she looked around with the appearance of nonchalance. 'Do you know if there's a restroom?'

'Through there.' He gestured to a double set of doors, bright red with portal windows.

'Thanks,' she murmured, reaching for her backpack casually, as though it were the most normal thing in the world, and excusing herself without a backwards glance. Her heart was racing so hard she thought it might give way as she slipped through the doors and into a corridor that had, she realised with relief, another door that led to a storeroom and then an alley.

Tears filled her eyes as she pushed through it and left the restaurant, her mind focused now on getting as far from Catarno as she possibly could.

But every step she took became harder and harder, heavier too, as if she were going in the wrong direction, wading through mud, pulling against elastic. Her lungs were burning with the force of breathing and her legs were shaking and as she pressed her back against a wall, waiting for her nerves to settle, she closed her eyes.

And saw him.

Benedetto, committed to memory perfectly, every inch of him, every beautiful, haunted, imperfect inch, and her heart stitched and her stomach rolled because the thought of never seeing him again was a torture she hadn't fully understood. She'd known it would be hard, but not akin to giving up breath or water. She'd thought she could control this. She'd thought she could spend time with him and not start to trust him, not start to want more from him. And maybe she could, but she wasn't ready to walk away from this yet.

'Damn it,' she muttered, dropping her head forward. What did that mean? She knew this would end. And soon—they were almost at Catarno. But she was running away again, and now she wasn't so sure it was the right choice. Everything was messy and confused, and it was all because of Benedetto. He'd got into her head and under her skin.

At first, he didn't think anything of it. He was more relaxed than he had been in years. Benedetto had always had an intensity about him, a wariness, courtesy of his father, and then their financial hardships. It was only a short time later he'd become a father, and that had probably been the only truly happy window of his life, a time when he'd gone from strength to strength professionally and had known, for the first time ever, uncomplicated, beautiful, easy love. He had loved his daughter with all of his heart, even when he would have said he didn't have a heart in the sense of feeling love. His had been just an organ responsible for pumping blood through his body until he'd met Sasha. Then he'd known what people were talking about. He'd loved her with all of himself, had known he would die before he let harm befall her.

And he would have.

If giving his life could have spared hers, Benedetto would have fallen upon the first sword he could find. But there had been no helping Sasha. He'd tried.

From that moment on, he'd been simply existing. Work had challenged him, had revived him, had brought him slowly back to life, and he'd taken a form of pleasure from succeeding, from rebuilding his fortune to the point of being one of the wealthiest men in the world, a Diamond Club member, welcomed into the most exclusive private club there was.

But everything had been about success. Not happiness, not relaxation, not enjoyment.

With Amelia, though, he'd felt a thousand things, not all of them good. He'd been aware of his conscience, he'd felt guilt, he'd felt shame, he'd felt frustration, even anger. But he'd also felt pleasure and joy, delight in another person's company. He'd felt things he couldn't quantify nor explain. And now, sharing a meal with her in a restaurant, which was such a normal activity, he'd felt relaxed despite what lay ahead for her, despite his worries for her and desire to shield her from any harm.

He'd let his guard down completely.

Which was why he hadn't noticed at first. He hadn't realised that she'd taken her bag. Hadn't been looking for anything out of the ordinary because he'd trusted her.

But just as he was starting to wonder why she was taking so long in the bathroom, his memory banged him over the head, reminding him of the image of her slipping through the door with the backpack over one shoulder. A backpack he hadn't even contemplated withholding despite the fact it had her phone, wallet and camera in it.

Because he trusted her.

Because he thought she felt—what? What did he want her to feel?

Had she expressed, at any point, a level of acceptance about going home?

Wasn't the opposite true? At every opportunity, whenever it came up, she insisted that it was wrong to go back. That she wouldn't forgive him for his part in it. That she couldn't face her family again.

He stood up quickly, reaching into his wallet, removing some money and throwing it onto the table before striding through the restaurant towards the doors to the restrooms.

The corridor was empty; a quick inspection of the stalls showed them to be likewise.

He felt as if he'd been stabbed in the chest.

He'd dropped his guard and Amelia had gone. Escaped. Left him.

Of course she had! He'd given her the perfect opportunity; could he blame her? The thought had even occurred to him but he'd dismissed it as ludicrous.

And if she wanted to avoid going home so badly, did he have any right whatsoever to chase her down again?

No.

He had no right.

He'd never had any right.

Amelia was a free agent. It was her life, her choice. She had to do what was right for her. Heart thumping hard against his ribs, he looked left and right, as if still hoping he might see her, before accepting that she had undoubtedly slipped far away from him already.

If she didn't want to be found, she wouldn't be.

* * *

They'd walked quite a way, and even with his long stride it was fifteen minutes before Benedetto made it back to the marina, to the boat he'd moored earlier that day with a strangely light heart. He grimaced as he stalked towards it and then stopped walking abruptly at the sight of the slim figure already on board, staring straight ahead. Frowning. Looking out to sea. Expression worried. Anxious.

His step quickened.

He stood short of the boat, staring at her, disbelief burning like acid in his gut. She turned to face him, her face mournful, confused, her eyes haunted, her cheeks stained with tears and he hated himself then for having anything to do with inflicting this pain on her.

'I'm sorry,' he said, moving quickly, stepping into the boat, crouching down before her. 'I should never have brought you here.'

She shook her head, evidently unable to speak. 'It's not Crete.'

'I don't mean Crete. I mean away from Valencia. I should never have got involved.'

A sob tore from her chest. He moved closer, cupping her face.

'You don't have to do this, Amelia. I'll take you home.'

'I don't know where home is,' she whispered. 'I don't know who I am.'

One of the deckhands approached their boat, looking to untether it, and protectiveness for Amelia, who was no longer in sunglasses or a hat, overrode everything else. He stood to shield her from view, slipped the deckhand a tip then sat beside her, ensuring she stayed out of view until they were alone again.

Even when they were, Benedetto remained where he was. 'Listen,' he said gently. 'This was a mistake. I didn't understand you, or the situation.' He put a hand on her leg, needing to feel her, to reassure her and also himself. He had to fix this. 'I'll take you back to Valencia.'

'You've already told Anton I'm coming.'

'I'll tell him I made a mistake. I'll tell him no one can force you to do anything you're not ready for. He'll be pissed—at me—but he'll get over it. Because it's the right thing to do. This should always have been your choice, Amelia. I apologise for not appreciating that sooner.'

She turned to look at him, her love-heart-shaped face so sorrowful that he groaned and pressed his forehead to hers. 'Please stop looking as though your world is ending. I made a mistake, but I'm going to fix it. It's going to be okay.'

'No, it's not,' she whispered, so haunted he wanted to stop the world and make everything and everyone in it do whatever was necessary to cause Amelia to smile. 'You don't know what you're talking about.'

He didn't. He had no idea what was going on, but he knew that forcing her to face it was wrong in a thousand kinds of ways. He could never be an instrument of pain to her. 'Come on,' he said softly, kissing her cheek with an odd, twisting feeling in the centre of his chest. 'Let's get you out of here.'

On the yacht, Amelia excused herself, numb to the core, needing to warm up with a shower. She stayed in there a long time, staring out of the darkly tinted window at the shore, imagining how things might have been now if she'd followed through with her escape. She'd formed a very quick plan as they'd wandered the streets, hand in hand, only hours earlier. She'd identified a travel agent, and located a bank, so she could access her trust fund.

There was no way to pull out money without revealing her identity but by the time any enterprising bank teller managed to sell the salacious information to a tabloid photographer, Amelia would have been long gone, booked onto a cruise ship off the island, where she would have stayed sequestered in her room until they put into port in a larger city, within reach of an airport.

And nobody would have been any the wiser.

But she hadn't been able to do it.

She missed her family. Even though she was terrified it might lead to heartbreak and pain for them, having come this close, the pull of Catarno and everything she'd walked away from was drawing her back, regardless of the risk.

And Ben? a voice in the back of her mind prompted. What role did he play in this? She tried to see through the wool in her mind, to understand. Their relationship still didn't mean anything. It was just temporary. But she would be lying to herself to pretend his offer to help hadn't lent strength to her. If the worst was to happen, was there anyone else she'd rather have at her side?

'What the hell do you mean?' Anton's voice came down the phone line with obvious surprise and Benedetto's hand tightened on the device.

'We're wrong to force her to come back.'

'You've got her on your boat, but you're saying you won't bring her to Catarno?' he repeated. 'Why the hell not?'

'She's adamant she can't come home.'

'This is where she belongs.'

'Then she'll come back of her own volition. It's not up to you or me to force her.'

'It's for her own good,' Anton snapped. 'You know the media circus that will erupt if she misses the wedding. Already the papers are full of speculation about it.'

'I know.' Benedetto nodded into the room. He'd seen the same reports. Not just the tabloids, even the broadsheets were running commentary on the likelihood of her return, speculating as to the work that was keeping her absent from royal life. 'And so does she. This has to be her decision, Anton.'

'You're serious?'

'I am.'

Anton swore softly. 'I trusted you.'

'And you still can. Trust me now—Amelia will always resent you if we do this. Would you rather she comes home for the wedding—and you lose her for ever—or that she returns when she's truly ready?'

'She will feel differently when she's here,' Anton said.

Benedetto closed his eyes. He owed Anton everything, but he should never have agreed to this. It was a family matter; Benedetto had no place getting involved. 'It has to be her decision, Anton. I'm not wrong about this.'

The Prince disconnected the call without another word.

CHAPTER EIGHT

HE FOUND HER in the underwater lounge room, staring out at the schools of fish, a book beside her, unopened, a cup of tea curled in her hands.

He hesitated in the doorway, not sure what to say, what to ask, what to do. It was an uncharacteristic uncertainty for Benedetto, and he resented it immediately.

'You turned the boat around.'

She'd clearly sensed him. He moved deeper into the room, then took the seat opposite her. 'Yes.'

Her eyes slid to his, pinned him to the spot. 'Why didn't I go through with it?'

He didn't pretend to misunderstand. 'I don't know.'

Her eyes glistened with unshed tears. 'I knew exactly what to do, how to escape, where to go. And then, I just couldn't do it. I couldn't.' A single tear slid down her cheek. She dashed it away quickly. 'Nothing makes sense.'

'Actually, I think things make sense for the first time all week. We're going back to Spain. That's the right choice. You can relax.'

Her smile was a shadow. 'Can I?'

'I've told Anton.'

Her brows shot up. 'What did he say?'

'Not a lot,' Benedetto responded truthfully. 'We had a slight difference of opinion on the matter, but he'll come round.'

'You're sure?'

'Yes, because I'm right.'

She shook her head slowly. 'You're right to leave the choice up to me, but I don't know what I should do. I hate the idea of going back, but how long am I going to stay away for? Am I really never going to see them again? And if I'm going to see them at some point, why not now?' She stood, teacup in hands, moving to the window, staring out at the fish without really seeing. 'I fought you tooth and nail but then today, when I could have left, I didn't. That has to say something about my subconscious mind, doesn't it?' Then, with eyes that were haunted and round like plates, she turned herself fully to face him. 'I miss them, Ben. I really miss them.' Another tear slid down her cheek, and he closed his own eyes, taking in a deep breath.

This was about her family, not him.

She'd come back for them, not because of Benedetto, and he was relieved because, despite the boundaries she'd insisted upon, a part of him was afraid that she was starting to want more than he could offer. Except she didn't. Nothing had changed.

'What do you want to do?'

That was a good question. She was standing on a precipice, and he was giving her the choice: to jump? Or not?

Amelia's eyes lifted to his and held, her throat shifting as she swallowed. 'I'm not who you think I am,' she said, eventually, so softly he almost didn't hear.

'What?'

Amelia pulled at a piece of invisible lint on her skirt and

then she sighed heavily. Was she really going to do this? The truth had been like a ticking time bomb inside her for a long time. She twisted her fingers anxiously, speaking without looking at Ben. 'About two and a half years ago, completely by accident, I found something out about myself.' Her brow furrowed, and she looked at him, then shook her head. 'I can't believe I'm telling you this.'

'You can trust me,' he said, as though he knew she needed to hear that.

'Can I?'

'Of course.'

He was right, she realised. Ben had turned the boat around. He hadn't wanted to, but, ultimately, he was a good person. He was doing what he saw was the morally correct thing. He would never use this information against her. He wasn't Daniel.

It was like a weight being lifted off her shoulders. She nodded tersely.

'I was looking for a picture book my mother used to read me as a child. I wanted to take it with me to a hospital visit, to read to sick kids; the book was always one of my favourites,' she said, remembering the day as though it were yesterday. 'The attic is one of the best places in the palace. We're not really meant to go there,' she explained. 'But even as a girl, I loved it. It's where all of our memories are packed away, neatly into boxes, archived for posterity's sake. There are these windows near the top of the walls, round and old, that let in just enough light to see all the dust motes dancing in the sunshine,' she said, tilting her head to the side. 'But there are lifetimes' worth of artefacts stored, so it's not easy to find one particular item. I started with a trunk marked books, and kept going. Occasionally, I would find a book that interested me, pull it out, read a few pages, put it back.'

Her brow furrowed; Benedetto remained quiet, giving her space to explain.

'And then, I found a paperback novel that almost seemed not to belong with the rest.'

'Didn't belong how?'

She waved a hand through the air. 'It just wasn't the kind of book you'd keep.' She shrugged. 'I was interested in why it was with the old leather-bound hardbacks. And when I opened it, an envelope fell out.'

Guilt flooded her heart, her chest, her cheeks flushed pink. 'I should have put it away without looking, but I was curious.'

'What was it?' Benedetto asked, leaning closer.

Amelia squeezed her eyes shut. 'On the front, it said simply *"darling"*. I had no idea what it would mean. I suppose I was captivated by the romance of it. But I knew the moment I opened the envelope and lifted out the photo that I'd discovered something important. And wrong.'

Benedetto's eyes roamed her face.

'It was a picture taken some years ago—twenty-three, as it turns out—of my mother with the head of our stables, a man named Felipe Lamart. It was an intimate photograph.' Amelia's cheeks darkened from pink to red, her eyes not meeting Ben's. 'And in the letter, he asked if she planned to keep their baby.'

Benedetto's breath hissed out from beneath his teeth.

'I'm the baby,' Amelia whispered, needlessly. 'The King isn't my father…my brothers are half-brothers. I'm evidence of an affair that my mother clearly wants to hide. My real father is Felipe Lamart—a man who, I discovered, died when I was ten years old. He never tried to contact me. Evidently he didn't want anything to do with me.' She shrugged, blinking away.

'This is why you ran away?'

She shook her head. 'I…was in a state of shock,' she mumbled, the words tripping over themselves. 'I shouldn't have said anything to anyone, but I couldn't make sense of it. I needed to talk to someone, to ask for advice. Or maybe I just wanted to get it off my chest, I don't know. It was an immense thing to have learned about myself.'

'Who did you tell?'

Amelia's anguish was profound. 'My boyfriend at the time, Daniel.'

Benedetto's voice was carefully muted of emotion. 'That's a very normal response. What did he say?'

'Nothing important. Not then. I decided to get a DNA test, just in case it was somehow a mistake. Daniel helped me organise it. We sent away to a lab in America, using Daniel's address for correspondence, so it couldn't easily be traced back to me.'

Benedetto nodded.

'The test confirmed what I'd discovered. The King and I don't share any DNA.'

Benedetto lifted a hand to her cheek. 'I'm sorry, *cara*.'

Amelia's voice trembled. 'Things hadn't been great with Dan and me for a while, and, after this, I just needed to be by myself. We broke up. I thought it was amicable, but I'd misunderstood.' She pushed to standing, striding across the room now, so angry with herself. 'I knew he was socially ambitious, that he didn't have much money and was capti-vated by the palace and the lifestyle, but I still thought… I really thought he was with me because he cared about me. I was so stupid, Ben. So stupid.'

'What happened?'

'He blackmailed me,' she whispered, fidgeting with her fingers. 'He had a copy of the DNA results. He said that if I didn't give him two million euros, he'd sell the story to the highest-bidding newspaper.'

Benedetto swore in Italian, crossing the room to stand right in front of Amelia.

'And so?'

'And so,' she repeated, aghast, 'everything would have been ruined. I'd discovered this awful secret of my mother's, and mine, something that could ruin her life, her marriage, could change everything for my family, and then I'd told someone who saw me as a paycheque. I couldn't believe how stupid I'd been.'

'It's not your fault.'

'Of course it is,' she contradicted. 'I should have known better.'

'You were in a state of shock.'

'Yes,' she muttered. At least that much was true. 'But that's no excuse.'

'What happened with Daniel?'

'I paid him. He said it would be enough, "for now".'

Benedetto swore beneath his breath.

'I felt like I would never be free of him, Ben.' She groaned. 'And so I disappeared. I thought with me gone, the risk would go too. And it has. But if I go back...'

Benedetto felt as though he'd been punched in the solar plexus. He stared at her long and hard, as the pieces slotted into place and he understood, finally, why she'd run away, how selfless and courageous she'd been in taking herself out of the palace, away from her parents, to protect her mother, to disappear rather than risk any of this coming out. And how terrified she must have been, how heartbroken, after her bastard ex-boyfriend's advantageous betrayal.

Something uneasy shifted inside Benedetto.

A sense that Amelia was vulnerable, that she'd been badly hurt. That despite what she'd said, if Benedetto wasn't very careful, this could come to mean more to her than he wanted. Because no matter how much he desired her, Benedetto had no intention of staying in Amelia's life. Or any woman's. He would never risk that kind of attachment, permanence, connection. Not after what he'd been through.

Every cell in his body was committed to a lifetime spent on his own, relying on no one, depending on no one, loving no one. Never again. He had to make sure Amelia didn't mistake his sympathy for anything else, especially not now he understood what she'd been through.

He wouldn't become another man who let her down.

'My whole life is a lie,' she mumbled, wrapping her arms around her chest. 'How could I keep going to family events, dinners, birthdays, Christmas, festivals, all the things we do together, knowing what I know, and what I'd done? And my father, the man who raised me and taught me to ride a bike and bake and laugh at corny old movies, how could I look him in the eye again?'

'He's still your father,' Benedetto said, keeping a careful distance between them.

'I don't belong with them. I don't belong anywhere.'

'Listen.' He spoke sternly, needing to cut through her sadness. 'What you learned, and how you learned it, was devastating. There's no excusing nor ignoring that. But it doesn't change the fact that your family loves you. None of this is your fault. Don't you think you should at least discuss the matter with your mother?'

Amelia gasped. 'I could never!'

'Why not?'

'She'd be devastated to know I know. And furious with me for turning to Daniel, of all people.'

'He was your boyfriend,' Ben said rationally. 'Trusting him makes sense.'

'Not for us. We were raised to be more careful than that. I should never have told another soul.'

'This is not your burden to carry,' he said emphatically. 'Your mother had an affair. That happens. It was a mistake. Decades later, she and your father are still together, happy. They've raised a family, are on the brink of watching their oldest son marry, presumably soon to welcome grandchildren into the mix. Life is long, if we're lucky, and not always as we expect it. Your father would understand. Your mother would certainly not want something she did two decades ago to keep you away a day longer.'

Amelia dropped her head to his chest and sobbed properly now, her grief shifting to something else, to a cathartic release, so Ben found it almost impossible not to react. But this was a vital moment. He would support her, but he needed to make sure their lines didn't get blurred.

'I don't want to go back to Valencia,' she said softly, eyes searching his, looking for answers. 'I don't know what to do next, but running away isn't going to fix this. It's not going to solve it.' She pulled back a little, looked up into his face. 'Will you take me to Catarno, Benedetto?'

It was the right choice. She needed to stop running, to be back with her family.

'Yes.'

She held his hand when he would have stepped away to issue the command to Cassidy and Christopher. 'But, Ben?' Her eyes were huge, filled with sadness. 'When we get there…' she pressed a hand to his chest '…this has to stop.'

It was exactly what he'd been thinking, wasn't it? That they needed to end this… So why did hearing her say that so factually aggravate him?

'It's going to be hard enough, dealing with all this. I don't need to worry about someone finding out we're sleeping together. My life at the palace is an open book. It would be too risky…'

'That makes sense,' he rushed to reassure her, relieved that it was Amelia who'd said it first. 'I'm there if you need me though,' he added. 'As a friend.'

Her smile was tight, and dismissive. He knew then that she wouldn't call on him for help, and he wondered why that bothered him so much.

The biggest port in Catarno was Livoa, where there was a high-security section used by the Catarno military and, when in use, the royal yacht. It was not a surprise to Amelia when Cassidy steered Benedetto's boat past the others and towards the high-security gates. There was no checking of identities—the information had been sent ahead, the serial number of the boat verified by computer—and they were waved past the armed guards, into a section of the marina that was heavily fortified.

Amelia shivered as the boat was brought to a stop. Beside her, Benedetto seemed to stiffen as well.

'If, at any point, you want to leave, I'm at your disposal.'

Her heart twisted uncomfortably, because she knew he meant it. He was her saviour after all. The problem for Amelia was that it made Benedetto pretty damned perfect, and all the emotions of hostility and anger she'd felt towards him initially, which had inured her from feeling anything more for him than wild, overpowering desire, had faded into nothing, so it was almost impossible not to let her heart get involved in things.

But that would be well and truly stupid.

Benedetto had done an about-turn; he had shown himself to be noble and good, but that didn't change the fact that he wasn't interested in a relationship. And knowing what she did about his upbringing and his loss as a father, she could understand why he'd chosen a life of solitude.

It would be really dumb to fall for him.

Really dumb.

And so she'd ended things pre-emptively, knowing that to keep going as they were was a one-way ticket to Disasterville, for Amelia at least.

She looked up at Benedetto and he smiled reassuringly, his face changing, morphing into something beautiful and breathtaking, and inwardly she groaned because, despite her very best intentions, she was pretty sure the horse had bolted on the whole love front already. 'It's going to be okay.'

It probably wouldn't, but, somehow, his words comforted her a little anyway.

As the boat putted along, then finally drew to a stop, she saw a limousine waiting with two flags on the front—her brother's crest, and the flag of Catarno.

Her heart dropped to her toes. 'I can't do this.'

'Yes, you can.'

She expelled a shaky breath but stood her ground, and because Benedetto was at her side, it felt easier, more practicable.

'Okay.' She nodded once. 'You're right. Let's go.'

Benedetto hadn't known what to expect. Flowers, serenades, her family lined up to greet her? Not this. The moment her feet connected with dry land, the royal guard formed a circle around her, separating Amelia from Benedetto, so she stared back at him wide-eyed, clearly terrified.

'Where are you taking her?'

None of them spoke to him and Amelia didn't say a thing in her own defence. The guards enveloped her so that, despite her height, she was almost invisible, and he understood—there was the risk of photographers lurking. They were protecting her.

Anger at his impotence—an unwanted and unwelcome feeling that reminded him what it had been like as a young boy hearing his mother berated and insulted—crested inside him. He was furious and powerless all at once as she was shepherded into the waiting limousine. He stared after it, already reaching for his phone to call Anton and demand an explanation, to demand he have the limousine turn back.

'Ben.'

He spun at the sound of his name to find his closest friend standing at the edge of the dock, watching proceedings with a grim expression. But then, Anton laughed softly, shaking his head. 'You look like you're about to punch something.'

Benedetto grimaced, schooling his expression into a

mask of calm. He was not his father. He would not surrender to anger. Ever.

'Your sister has done an incredibly brave thing. I intended to escort her to the palace, to make sure she was okay.' Even to his own ears, it sounded stupidly defensive.

'What for?' Anton's eyes narrowed. 'And brave how? She's come home, Ben, not to face a firing squad, but to be welcomed back with open arms by all and sundry. What in the world is she so afraid of?'

To that, Benedetto could not reply truthfully.

'Where are they taking her?'

'To my mother, who has not slept for two days, since I told her that Amelia was coming home. We deliberated a long time about the best way to effect the reconciliation and decided privacy was appropriate.'

Ben heard the subtext. This was a family matter.

'Come on.' Anton nodded over his shoulder, to where another car was waiting. 'Ride with me.'

A whole kaleidoscope of butterflies had taken up residence inside Amelia as the limousine cut through the streets of the old city and took the mountain roads to the palace. So familiar to her, so stunning and unlike any other part of the world. She could only stare out of the window—flanked as she was on either side by a guard, as though even now there was a risk she'd bolt—and allow the memories to consume her.

When the palace came into view, it was a moment of intense pain and exuberance. She made a guttural gasping sound and turned, seeking Benedetto, wanting to share it with him, but not able to, because he was no longer with her.

And that wasn't his fault.

The guard had descended too quickly, had taken her away, and she'd let them. She could have commanded them to stop, to wait for him, but part of her had been glad to separate, because she'd made the decision to part from him. Self-preservation instincts had kicked in.

Running away again? a little voice demanded, but she ignored it.

If she was running away, it was only because it was the right thing to do. Benedetto wouldn't want her to develop serious feelings for him—he'd sprint in the opposite direction if he thought there was any risk of that. Better to have ended it now, before it started to mean something to Amelia. Before she started to want him in her life, for always and for ever...

The limousine approached the palace gates, paused and entered at a snail's pace before picking up speed again. The trees to the west of the path were in full bloom, startlingly yellow and so beautiful her heart lifted despite the trepidation she felt. The palace itself was a sight she'd craved, and Amelia drank it in now, every stone face and gold-tipped turret, the wall that was covered in scrambling bougainvillea, the roses that grew rampant at the front of the palace. It was all so lovely, so utterly known to Amelia.

Nervousness besieged her but somehow there was also relief. She could barely keep her emotions in check as she stepped from the vehicle, looking around on autopilot for Benedetto. But of course he wasn't there yet.

She turned to one of the guards. 'Would you have a car sent to the dock to collect Benedetto di Vassi?'

'He has been collected, Your Highness.'

She physically recoiled at the use of her title. It had been a long time.

'Is he here?' She cursed her weakness immediately for asking the question.

'This way please, Your Highness.' Another guard spoke swiftly, a woman, gesturing towards the palace. Amelia compressed her lips, frustrated, but also impatient now, because she gathered where this was going. She was being brought home, to her family, to meet with them away from any risk of public scrutiny.

Her nerves jangled as the guard led her through the palace, as if she wouldn't know the way herself, to the doors of one of the morning rooms.

'Her Majesty is waiting,' the female guard said with a small bow before opening the door and ushering Amelia in.

And there was her mother, standing in the middle of the room, wringing her hands in the exact same way Amelia did when she was nervous, until she saw Amelia and let out a cry that was barely human and ran across the room, throwing her arms around her daughter.

'Oh, my darling,' she sobbed, burying her head in Amelia's shoulder, crying so much that her body was racked and her face wet. 'You're home. You have no idea how badly I wanted this, how much I have missed you. Oh, my darling, my darling girl, let me look at you,' and she pulled away only so she could study Amelia intently for several seconds before wrapping her up in another huge hug.

Amelia was numb and overwhelmed at the same time, an unusual combination but so it was. She'd missed her mother too, and she loved her so much, but she knew that she had to grow strong, to inure herself to this life, because it wasn't tenable for her to stay. She didn't belong here. She didn't belong anywhere.

Except on the boat, with Benedetto, that same dangerous little voice whispered in the back of her mind, imploring her to listen, to escape again, but this time, with him. This time with the proper goodbyes to her family, so they wouldn't worry. But that was a fantasy she couldn't indulge; it would never work long-term—he wouldn't want it, and she couldn't bear to ask it of him.

'My darling, tell me everything.' Anna-Maria Moretti wiped her tears and gestured to a small floral-covered sofa. They sat down as the door opened and a servant carried through a tray of biscuits and tea.

'"Everything" would take a while.'

'We have a while, don't we?' Anna-Maria asked, eyes roaming her daughter's face. 'You're not going anywhere, are you?'

Amelia couldn't quite meet her mother's eyes. 'Mum, listen,' she began cautiously. But what could she say? That she knew about the affair? About her parentage? That she'd been blackmailed, that someone out there knew their secret? She clamped her mouth shut.

'It's okay, it's okay. You're home now. We can talk about it later.'

'Okay,' Amelia agreed, uneasily though, anxious, stressed, worried, of all people, about Benedetto. Who was more than capable of looking after himself.

She expelled a long, slow breath.

'Tell me about Anton's fiancée. Tell me what I've missed.'

Relieved that it seemed Amelia wasn't going to disappear immediately, Anna-Maria began to speak, a little too quickly, as though she too was uneasy, or nervous, but gradually she calmed.

'She's wonderful, you'll love her. We all do. She's been

so good for Anton, so calming and steadying. She's made him a better man.'

'How did they meet?'

'At a hospital benefit. She's a paediatrician, you know. She'll give it up, once they're married, which is a great shame, but the constitution demands it.' Anna-Maria tsked her disapproval. 'Your father tried to change it but apparently he cannot. Sadly for Vanessa, she'll have to content herself with some volunteer work and becoming a patron of the charities she likes.'

'Is she okay with that?'

'I think it took some getting used to, which is one of the reasons she refused his proposal the first two times.' Anna-Maria's brows knitted together. 'She had a difficult upbringing, you know, to her, we are already like parents. I hope you like her, darling. I know it will mean so much to her to have you as a sister. She's been so looking forward to meeting you.'

Amelia's chest was hurting. She felt terrible for having disappeared, for having worried everyone, for having missed so much, and she also felt awful for being back, for the risk her appearance brought to them, for the possibility that just by being here she was exposing the family to a scandal from which they might not recover. She was a living, ticking time bomb, her very life the evidence of her mother's affair. Amelia was the evidence, but it was her mother who'd cheated, then lied, and as Amelia sat opposite the Queen, she couldn't help but feel a whip of anger at the base of her spine.

'I'm looking forward to meeting her too,' Amelia promised, distracted now.

Anna-Maria spent an hour going over everything else

Amelia had missed and also some scheduling concerns, such as the dress fitting for the wedding, and the requirements for the next few days. Amelia barely paid attention.

'From tomorrow, the official events will commence. You arrived just in time, darling. Just in time.' Then, with a softening to her face and a hint of moisture back in her eyes, she said, 'I'm just so glad you came home. You have no idea how much I've missed you.'

'I've missed you too,' Amelia whispered, and, despite the complex emotions she felt towards her mother, she knew that was right.

As they hugged, the door opened and His Majesty King Timothy Moretti strode into the room, dressed formally, followed by his second son, Rowan. 'Good God, it's true,' Timothy said, wiping a hand over his eyes. 'You're home.'

A lump formed in Amelia's throat as she faced the moment she'd feared the most—seeing again the man who'd raised her, knowing he was not her father, that he'd been duped into the role. And though it had not been her lie, her betrayal, nor her fault, guilt curdled her gut and nausea rose like a tidal wave inside her.

She bowed, as was custom, but the King made a noise of frustration and pulled her into his arms, hugging her so hard she thought a rib might crack. 'Don't you ever, ever do anything like this again,' he said fiercely, but with a voice that shook. 'I forbid it. By royal decree, do you understand?' It was a joke, of sorts, but Amelia heard the strain in his voice and again the guilt at having run away and hidden herself from her family crashed into her like a tonne of bricks. What else could she have done though? She felt risk from every angle; it was stupid to have come back, but how could she have stayed away? Amelia felt as though she were caught between a rock and a hard place.

'I've missed you,' she said, simply, because she could not promise to stay, but had truly yearned for her family. A moment later, Rowan hugged her and her heart skipped because she felt closest of all to her middle brother, who'd had the privilege of growing up royal without the pressures.

'Ready to be one of us again?' he asked lightly, his eyes scanning her face.

Amelia swallowed quickly; she wasn't one of them, though. 'I'm glad to see you all.'

Rowan's eyes narrowed but he didn't push it, and Amelia was glad. There were some answers she just didn't have yet.

Benedetto had been to the palace before but now he saw it through different eyes. He saw it as the place where Amelia had grown up, the gardens she'd run through, the art she'd studied, the long, historic, beautiful corridors she'd skipped down as a child. The building that had housed her heartbreaks, hopes, that had finally borne witness to her awful discovery and the impact that had on her, the blackmail, the pain of that betrayal.

'You're not listening,' Anton said with a grin, a study in relaxed calm now that Amelia was back and Benedetto had taken his place at Anton's side.

'No.' Benedetto was unapologetic. 'Tell me again.'

'You're still worried about her.'

Benedetto's eyes flashed to Anton's. 'Yes.'

'You're being ridiculous. She's fine. Probably just being suffocated by my parents' many, many embraces.'

'Aren't you eager to see her too?' Benedetto asked, his voice carefully muted of emotion.

'I haven't seen her in over two years. I can wait a little longer.'

'You're angry with her.'

'It's my wedding in three days,' Anton said, but now Benedetto saw through the air of relaxation. 'I'm not angry about anything.'

Benedetto was too good a study of dark emotions though. 'Why?' he pushed.

Anton compressed his lips, gave up the pretence. 'Why do you think?' He spread his hands outward. 'She broke my mother's heart. And kept breaking it, every day she stayed away, every message she did not respond to, every time she refused to see us. Each Christmas and birthday she missed. She's selfish, Ben. Yes, I'm angry with her. But I can't think about that now, because in three days I'm getting married in a ceremony that will be broadcast across the globe, and viewed in person by thousands, including the heads of state of most countries in the world. So Amelia is the furthest thing from my mind.'

CHAPTER NINE

'LOOKING FOR SOMEONE?'

Despite her older brother's insufferable arrogance, she was surprisingly glad to see him. She turned to face Anton, not sure what greeting to expect from the sibling who was much older than her, far more serious, and incredibly dedicated to his duties.

'No,' she denied, only realising when Anton asked the question that she had been wandering the corridors of the palace in the hope of seeing Benedetto. Even though she'd ended things between them, she still wanted to *see* him, and she couldn't explain why.

'You put us all through hell, you know,' Anton murmured, standing in front of her, his autocratic face wiped of emotion.

She should have expected this from Anton. A lecture. After all, he had been the one to send Ben, to tell him everything about Amelia, and Ben had clearly thought the worst of her initially.

'It's good to see you too.'

He paused. 'I am glad you're home.'

'Well, you made sure of that, didn't you? At least I can add being kidnapped to the bucket-list items I've ticked off.'

'My understanding is you chose to return of your own free will, when the option was given to you.'

So Anton and Ben had discussed it? What else had they spoken about? Her pulse ratcheted up a gear.

'It seems as though my friend has become your knight in shining armour.'

Amelia's cheeks flushed a telltale pink but she worked hard to maintain a neutral expression. She wouldn't be drawn on what Ben had become to her. How could she answer that anyway, when she didn't even know herself?

'He told me what you did for him,' she said instead. 'When Sasha died. That was very kind of you, Anton, very decent.'

Anton stared at her long and hard. 'He told you about Sasha?'

Amelia stiffened. Had she inadvertently revealed more about their relationship than she'd intended anyway? 'A week on a boat is a long time,' she pointed out. 'We talked about a lot of stuff.'

'Sasha isn't stuff, she's— He doesn't open up about it. Ever. Maybe because you're my sister,' Anton reasoned, 'he presumed you already knew.'

Amelia let that settle between them, lifted her shoulder. 'Perhaps.' And something about his egotistical presumption endeared him to her, so she closed the distance between them, pressed a kiss to his cheek. 'I'm glad to see you, even though you drive me crazy.'

He lifted one dark brow. 'Do I?'

'Yes. Now, when do I get to meet your fiancée? I hear she's got the patience of a saint.'

At that, Anton laughed softly. 'I know you're teasing

me, but in fact, you're right. Vanessa is—beyond compare. She'll be at dinner tonight.'

'Dinner?'

'Just the family.'

Amelia's heart sank. *I'm not family*, she wanted to scream. But how could she avoid this? What could she possibly say? And at least Benedetto wouldn't be there. For as much as she wanted to see him, from a distance at least, she wasn't sure she could trust herself to be in the same room as him and act as though he meant nothing to her.

Avoiding him was a far better idea.

As soon as Benedetto saw Amelia, he wanted to stop the clock and wind back time, he wanted to remove every last vestige of her princess life and return her to the wild, free spirit she'd been on his yacht, with hair all tousled and windswept, skin warm from the sun, face bare of make-up, clothes loose and floaty in concession to the heat, feet almost always bare. He wanted to go back to before she'd told him they should stop seeing each other and kiss the words right out of her mind. He just wanted to kiss her...

This Amelia was so different. Despite the fact it was a 'quiet family dinner', she was dressed to the nines. This was Her Royal Highness Princess Amelia Moretti, and she was every inch the princess indeed.

From hair that had been styled until it shone and pinned into an elegant bun low on her head, to the dainty tiara she wore, the suit—cream with gold buttons, she'd teamed a blazer with trousers and wore brown high heels that were the same shade as the small handbag she carried. Her face had been made up expertly, and at her throat she wore a simple necklace with a single diamond in the centre.

It was the first time they'd seen each other since being separated at the boat and curiosity had him staring at her intently across the room, waiting for her to notice him, but she was locked in conversation with Vanessa, who wore a pale pink gown with her dark hair loose around her face.

Frustration champed at Benedetto. He feigned interest in conversation with Rowan—who he usually liked and had a lot of time for. But at that very moment, all of his focus was absorbed by Amelia. She moved eventually from Vanessa to her mother, speaking in a low voice, smiling, laughing, and it was when she laughed that she tilted her head and her eyes met his.

Every muscle in his body tightened. The breath in his lungs caught and held. His lips parted on a short hiss of air and he had never before known a temptation quite like it: to storm across the room, throw her over his shoulder and run away with Amelia.

He forced himself to look away, back to Rowan, to nod at something he'd said, to actively listen to the conversation now, but he was conscious of her the whole time, and in the back of his mind he was planning ahead, attempting to work out how to peel Amelia away from her family, so he he could be alone with her.

Except he couldn't. Or shouldn't.

She was right to have put an end to what they were doing. He'd be crazy to pursue her now, here in the palace. Her life was an open book, as she'd said. That didn't stop him from wanting her though, and from needing to know she wanted him too...

Just being back with her family was exhausting. They were all making an effort to be accepting, no one asking her about her prolonged, unexplained absence, but she felt the questions, the judgement, the low-key anger and resentment from Anton. Or perhaps it was just the secret knowledge she held that she didn't really belong here, that she wasn't a real princess, that was playing on her mind.

Beneath the table, she fidgeted with her fingers, twisting the large diamond ring she wore, a gift from her grandmother, who had also clearly had no idea that Amelia was an imposter in their midst.

And the one person who had the power to make her feel better, to blot out all of this tension, was as far as physically possible across the table, and being monopolised in conversation by her father and Rowan. When their eyes had met, she'd felt a surge of awareness and known she couldn't look in his direction again. It would be too obvious. Surely someone would notice. And so she concentrated hard on being what everyone expected her to be, on smiling and nodding and ignoring Benedetto with every fibre of her being.

The night was long. Several courses, speeches, more food, and, finally, Anton signalled the evening was at an end by excusing himself and Vanessa. With immense relief, Amelia looked around, her eyes instantly latching to Benedetto's. He was watching her and the moment she felt his gaze on her, felt it connect with hers, her stomach squeezed and her heart stammered.

'Goodnight, darling,' her mother murmured, leaning over and placing a kiss on her forehead. Then, 'Tomorrow is going to be very busy, but if you'd like to join me for a walk in the morning, I'll be leaving from the West Gate at six.'

A smile pulled at Amelia's lips. For as long as she could remember, her mother had been conducting the same early morning walk through the gardens, past the stables, and down to the citrus grove. Amelia had often walked with her as a teenager.

'Thank you,' she said, without committing either way. 'Goodnight.'

Amelia stood, but rather than leaving the room, she moved deeper into it, pretending fascination with a painting on the wall. It was hundreds of years old, a Biblical scene with angels and clouds and women reclining with their long hair draped over their bodies.

Her heart raced as she studied the painting and listened as her family slowly filtered from the room, and she held her breath, waiting, hoping. She knew the smart thing to do would be to depart likewise. She'd ended things with Benedetto for a reason—it couldn't keep going on—but that didn't mean she had suddenly turned into a robot. She *wanted* to see him. She *wanted* to talk to him, to be alone with him.

The room was silent for such a long time that her heart plummeted, because Benedetto must have left too and the hope she'd nurtured all night of finally being alone with him withered into nothingness.

She turned, fidgeting with her ring, and then let out a small gasp, because he hadn't left at all. He was sitting at the table, staring straight ahead, a small coffee cup in his big, strong hands. Her heart skipped a beat and she moved to him as though being pulled by strings, gliding across the ancient carpets.

'Hello.'

He turned to face her, his expression inscrutable.

'How are you?'

It was a question laced with far greater meaning than

the words usually asked for. He was asking how she really was. Not in the trivial sense, but in the deep emotional sense after all she'd been through today.

'It was tough,' she said, honestly.

'Are you glad you came back?'

She shook her head. 'I don't know.' Then, looking around the table, 'It wouldn't have felt right to miss it.'

'No,' he agreed. Then he stood, meeting her eyes, and her breath hitched in her throat, fear surging inside her. Was he going to leave? 'They care about you a great deal.'

'I know.' Her voice cracked. She didn't want to discuss her family. 'How's your day been?'

'Honestly?'

She nodded.

'Long.'

Amelia scanned his face. 'I presumed Anton was keeping you busy.'

'Yes, extolling the virtues of his fiancée, which I've heard about a thousand times, mind you.'

'He's madly in love.' Amelia smiled, but there was a strange hollowness in her heart as she spoke those words. Suddenly, not being able to touch him was a form of torture, and yet she'd done this to herself. 'Benedetto—'

'Amelia,' he returned, drawling her name with a hint of mockery.

She toyed with the ring she wore. 'This is weird.'

'Being back in Catarno?'

'Being here with you.'

His eyes flared. 'You are not with me.'

'No.' Her voice was ambivalent.

'You can't be,' he reminded her, or perhaps he was reminding himself too. 'It's too complicated.'

Amelia nodded, but frowned. 'Maybe it doesn't have to be.'

Benedetto was very still. 'Go on.'

'There's a way to my room through my office. You could come to me tonight.'

His nostrils flared. 'Sneak around behind your family's back?'

Heat flushed her cheeks. 'I know it's not ideal...'

'I'm not a teenager, Amelia, and neither are you.'

'My personal life is no one's business,' she said, tightly, but she was hurt, because he'd rejected her.

'You were the one who said your life here is an open book,' he pointed out.

'I know. It is. But—'

'There is no but,' he said, with a single shake of his head. 'We can't do this.'

'Damn it.' She stomped her foot, but at that moment a team of servants burst through the doors, intent on clearing the table. Amelia's eyes met Benedetto's, held them, her lips parted but what more could she say?

'Goodnight, Your Highness,' he said, with a dip of his head.

Amelia's heart turned cold. 'Goodnight,' she whispered, but Benedetto had already left.

If she hadn't told him about the discreet access to her room, he wouldn't have been lying in bed for hours, hard as a rock, staring at the ceiling, thinking of Amelia, craving her, wanting, wishing, needing.

But she had, and he was, and at some point in the small hours of the morning, tired of wanting and not having, he gave up on being noble and right, and decided to give into temptation. One more time. It still didn't mean anything. It was just sex. Like on the boat, but here. What did geography matter? So long as they both understood the temporary nature of this, what was the harm?

Benedetto dressed in a pair of trousers and a shirt, slipped his feet into shoes and strode from his room, down the corridor, towards the suite of rooms he knew, from previous visits, belonged to Amelia.

He concealed a bitter smirk as he approached her doors. One wrong turn and he might very well end up in Anton's rooms instead. How to explain that? he thought. But his memory was accurate. Silently, he pushed the heavy oak door inwards, taking in the details of Amelia's study as he went—the floral paintings, the pretty furniture, the large windows. He closed the door then looked around, for another way into and out of the room. At first, he missed it. This doorway was only three-quarter height, a relic from a different century, when people were smaller.

He moved to it, hand on the doorknob, as he contemplated turning back.

There were a thousand reasons to resist Amelia, namely, because he wanted to be able to look back and know that he'd acted honourably towards her. That he'd never done anything to risk her heart.

Which brought him back to the necessity of being honest with her *before* this happened.

So long as she understood, this would all be okay.

He knocked on the door lightly, then realised how stupid that was—she was probably asleep. So he probably shouldn't interrupt her. He should probably just go back to his room, stick to his original, much wiser idea, to ignore Amelia altogether.

'Yes?' Her voice was small, but audible.

His gut churned and his body tightened.

There was no way he was turning back.

He pushed the door inwards, frustration bursting through him. It was a frustration aimed mostly at himself, because he should have been strong enough to resist her. But it was also aimed at Amelia, because she'd invited him here. She'd weakened too.

'This is a terrible idea,' he muttered, striding across to the edge of her bed and staring down at her, wishing she didn't look so beautiful and innocent with her knees pulled up to her chest.

'What is?' Her eyes were huge in her face. It was dark in the room, except for the full moon's beam streaking through the window. He reached down, touched her cheek, felt his body galvanise with need.

He ignored her question. She'd asked him here for one reason; he'd come because of that.

'You understand—' He paused, scanning her face in the silver light. She looked up at him, guarded, careful, uncertain.

Benedetto cursed inwardly.

'I'm leaving as soon as the wedding's over,' he said. 'We won't see each other again.'

She was still. He waited, on tenterhooks. 'I know that.'

'You understand what I'm offering.'

Her lips pulled to the side in a gesture that was now intimately familiar to him. 'Sex,' she murmured, and then moved to kneeling, so their faces were almost at a level. 'The perfect, meaningless distraction,' she added as she leaned forward and kissed him, and Benedetto relaxed into the moment, because she *did* understand. There was no risk here. No complication. Just perfect, meaningless, satisfy-ing sex, for a few more nights, and then he'd leave without a backwards glance, just like always.

Amelia woke early, stretching in the bed, frowning when she couldn't discern the familiar rhythms of the boat's rock-ing, then remembering the reason for that. She was no lon-ger aboard *Il Galassia*, but rather here, in the palace, her home, with her family. And Benedetto.

Her skin flushed as she remembered the way he'd made love to her the night before, his desperate need, his body so strong and commanding, so capable, hard and perfect for her. The way he'd kissed her to muffle her screams, how he'd laced their fingers together and lifted her arms over her head to stop her from touching as he simply moved inside her, stirring her to a fever pitch, pleasing her again and again until she could barely breathe, much less speak or remember who or where she was.

Her body had felt both weak and strong afterwards, legs made of jelly, heart of steel. He'd turned to her, as if try-ing to ascertain something in her features, and then pushed to standing. Magnificent in his nakedness, glorious and sensual.

'You're leaving?'

He'd dipped his head once in silent agreement.

Her heart had felt momentarily hollow, but she concealed that reaction. 'It's probably for the best. There's no point letting anyone find out about this when it's so temporary.'

'My thoughts exactly.'

The air had pulsated between them. 'So it's our secret,' she'd said, a rush of excitement exploding in her veins.

Benedetto hadn't wanted to sneak around like a teenager, yet there they were, making exactly that sort of pact. 'Yes,' he'd agreed after a small pause. 'I'll see you soon.'

She'd wanted to ask when, but had, thankfully, stopped herself. She wouldn't reveal any kind of neediness to him. It was the last thing he'd want, and when the wedding was over and Benedetto was gone, and Amelia had moved on, she'd be proud of herself for seeming so casual.

'She's been very good for him, you know,' Anna-Maria said as they approached the crest of the hill and wound their way around the precipice, to reach a point with one of the most spectacular views of the valley. It was still early and the sun was only just cresting over the hills in the distance, casting the sky in the most spectacular oranges and pinks.

'In what way?' Amelia prompted, pausing to sip her water.

'He's far less serious. Oh, I love Anton, of course, but he can be a little intense sometimes,' Anna-Maria said with a wink.

'Mum!'

Anna-Maria linked her hand through Amelia's arm. 'You know what I mean. It's been hard for him, having the weight of his inheritance on his shoulders, knowing all his life that he would become King. Vanessa makes him laugh at himself, makes him laugh with the rest of us. And she helps him. She's very smart, an excellent sounding board for all manner of things. The public adores her too.'

Something like jealousy flashed in Amelia's gut and she turned away to conceal the bitterness from showing on her face. It wasn't the public who'd had issues with her though, but the press who'd seemed to delight in painting her as the misfit third child, who'd tormented her through their stories and lies. And the public had bought the papers and magazines, had believed so much of it. Amelia sighed softly.

Perhaps sensing the direction of Amelia's thoughts, Anna-Maria softened her tone. 'They never really gave you a fair shot, did they?'

'No.' Amelia flattened the hurt from her voice.

'I wish I'd known how to protect you better from that. At the time, I thought we were doing the right thing, by telling you to ignore it. But that wasn't fair. I should have done more.'

Amelia compressed her lips, neither agreeing nor disagreeing. Her parents had been in a difficult position—the royal family never commented on stories in the press. It was a policy of long standing. But the thick skin needed to cope with the onslaught of publicity was something Amelia had never really developed.

'Is that why you left?' Anna-Maria prompted gently.

'No,' Amelia murmured, sipping her water. 'But I'm not going to lie to you, the lack of press coverage over the last couple of years has been astoundingly nice. The silence has been wonderful.'

'I can imagine,' Anna-Maria agreed.

Amelia angled her face towards her mother's as they began to walk once more, arm in arm. 'You married into this lifestyle. Have you ever regretted it?'

'I always knew I would marry him and become Queen,' she said with a lift of her shoulders. 'Your father and I were betrothed when I was just a girl and he a boy. It was my destiny, and his, arranged by our parents to strengthen the throne and the royal family's place in the country's political system. My family was politically very powerful, his royal. It made sense.'

'I never knew that,' Amelia said with genuine surprise. 'You're saying your whole life you've been living in an arranged marriage?'

'Well, yes,' Anna-Maria agreed, as if she too was a little surprised to have revealed as much.

'But you seem—I thought you guys had fallen in love. I knew your family was powerful, I just presumed you'd come to know one another by moving in the same circles.'

'And so we did.'

'But you didn't marry for love?' Amelia asked breathlessly, piecing together an entirely different visage of her mother's life.

Her lips twisted. 'I married for love, in some ways,' Anna-Maria said hesitantly. 'I loved my parents, my country. I loved the idea of being Queen, particularly the jewels and gowns,' she added with another wink. 'And I liked and respected your father a great deal.'

Amelia's footing slipped a little at the mention of her father.

'But love took time with us. We fell in love on the job, so to speak.'

'So you do love him now?'

'Very much.'

'What made you love him?' Amelia pushed, her voice heavy with interest.

Was she imagining the way her mother's skin paled a little?

'Some time ago, when the boys were little and you were not yet born, a series of events led me to realise that I couldn't live without him,' she said. 'It was that simple. I had fallen in love without even realising it, and only when I thought about what I could lose, if I didn't face up to how

I felt, did I finally comprehend the strength of my own feelings. I fell in love with him gently, softly, while I wasn't even paying attention, and for a thousand different reasons. I loved him for his passion for the arts—music, theatre, opera. His skill as a polo player. His body,' she added, knocking her hip into Amelia's, to signal a joke, but Amelia could hardly catch her breath, much less smile. This insight into her parents' marriage, given what she knew, was destabilising, to say the least.

'I loved how much he thought about everything. Your father is never rash, always considerate, he looks at a problem from every conceivable angle, sometimes twice, before responding. He's incredibly smart. And over time, he fell in love with me too.' Anna-Maria stopped walking, turned to face her daughter.

'You've been gone so long, I feel as though I have to get to know you all over again, in some ways.' She squeezed Amelia's forearm. 'Tell me, have you been in love, Amelia?'

'No,' she answered, but not entirely without hesitation. She'd thought she'd loved Daniel, but that had been a mistake. And since then, there'd been only Benedetto. While she lusted after him around the clock, that wasn't the same thing as love.

'Ah. I wasn't sure. I thought perhaps in Spain, you might have met someone.'

'No. No one.'

'That's a shame.'

'Is it?'

'Of course. But one day, you will find your other half, and you'll understand, when you love that person, that the idea of losing them suddenly becomes a form of torture. It wasn't just the thought of losing your father that made me realise how much I loved him, but the idea of jeopardising our family.'

'And so you realised you loved him, and then I was born,' Amelia said, studying her mother with every ounce of her concentration, looking for any hint of emotion that might betray the truth of Amelia's parentage.

But Anna-Maria smiled beatifically and nodded. 'You were a living, breathing testament to our love. A reminder every day of how much our marriage meant to us both, of why we would always fight for it, and each other.'

Amelia let out a soft breath. Was that true? Could she be both evidence of an illicit affair and a talisman to faithfulness? If what her mother was saying was true, and Amelia could read between the lines because she had a greater knowledge of the subject than her mother realised, was it possible that by cheating on the King, and recognising that her affair would potentially end her marriage, she decided to recommit herself to the King, to love him properly and fully? It made sense. In which case, Amelia supposed she could have been just what Anna-Maria had described.

'One day, you will fall in love, just as Anton has, and I will look forward to meeting the person who captures your heart.' She put an arm around Amelia. 'You are so special, darling. No matter what, don't forget that.'

CHAPTER TEN

'OH, WHAT A SURPRISE,' Anton remarked under his breath. 'Amelia's late.'

Something shifted inside Benedetto, an irritation, an impatience, a quickness to judge he'd never felt towards his friend. He tried to suppress it, but when Anton looked at Benedetto with a grin, Benedetto didn't return it. If anything, his expression was ice cold.

'She'll be here,' Anna-Maria said. 'And in the meantime, let's carry on.'

The rehearsal was long and involved and as Benedetto was to stand with his best friend as a groomsman, alongside Rowan, who was best man, he was an integral part of proceedings. But so was Amelia.

Where was she?

Far from taking the cynical tone of voice his friend had adopted, he felt worry begin to fray at the edges of his mind. She wouldn't have run away again, he was sure of it, but it also seemed strange that she'd be late for something as important as this. He gave the rehearsal about a tenth of his focus and spent the rest of his time looking at his watch surreptitiously and kicking himself for not having taken her phone number in exchange for giving out his own.

'This is where the bridesmaid will take the bouquet.'

'If she shows up,' Anton drawled, earning a sharp gaze from his mother and a placating hand on the arm from his fiancée. At that exact moment, the doors to the chapel opened and a clearly flustered Amelia jogged in.

'You've already started,' she said as she drew near the group.

'Yes, an hour ago, when the rehearsal was scheduled for,' Anton sniped.

'My schedule says three o'clock,' she responded tersely, brandishing her phone. 'And I've literally just got out of the dress fitting. Why did no one call me?'

They all looked at each other, but when Amelia's eyes came to Benedetto, he hoped she could see how proud he was of her for speaking up to Anton.

'Oh, dear.' Vanessa spoke first, moving to Amelia and looking at her phone. 'You've been sent the old timetable. I'm so sorry, that's our mistake completely.' Benedetto liked Vanessa more and more. 'There have been so many changes in the last week, everything's tweaked and you've received the schedule that was valid up until a couple of days ago.'

'It's fine.' Amelia's manner softened immediately in deference to her future sister-in-law, and perhaps in response to the obviously conciliatory tone in Vanessa's voice. 'I'm sorry to have missed so much.'

'Oh, it's nothing complicated. I'll have a printed guide sent to your room, but other than walking in with me, and taking my bouquet, the main thing is to stand at my side and smile serenely.'

'That I think I can manage,' Amelia replied. There were smiles all round, except from Benedetto, who had a deluge of unfamiliar emotions cresting in his belly.

After the rehearsal, when Benedetto wanted nothing

more than to leave with Amelia, and ideally whisk her back to the boat for a few hours of actual privacy, he couldn't even get close enough to her to speak. Frustration bubbled beneath his skin as he watched her disappear into a limousine, bookended by the King and Queen.

She suddenly seemed incredibly untouchable, and he hated that...

Amelia's feet were killing after a full day spent in heels, which she hadn't worn for the longest time. In fact, she'd barely worn closed-toe shoes at all since leaving Catarno. She flicked on the TV in her room, smiling at the footage that came up of Anton and Vanessa meeting well-wishers outside the palace. They were a very handsome couple and Anna-Maria was right—Vanessa was clearly an excellent match for Anton.

Amelia was on her way to the bathroom to fill the tub when a knock sounded at her door. Not the main door, but the smaller door from her study. With an unsteadiness to her legs suddenly, she crossed the room and wrenched it inwards, smiling instinctively at the sight of Benedetto on the other side.

His eyes flared with hers and before she could make a joke about the contortions he had to perform to get through the space, he was in her room and dragging her into his arms, kissing her hard, fast, slamming the door shut with his foot and fumbling the lock before lifting her, legs cradled around his waist, and carrying across the room.

She squawked as he dropped her onto the mattress then felt breathless when he simply studied her as though she were a piece of delicate artwork. Her pulse quickened.

She pushed up, reaching for him, as he came towards her,

and their bodies melded once more, twisting together, legs, arms, lips meshed, hearts racing, clothes being shucked with so much urgency that something made a ripping noise and Amelia laughed softly, but only for a minute, because then he was taking her, and it was more, so much more, than she'd ever known. His possession of her was so fierce and absolute, so breathtakingly swift, so full of hungry need that something powerful seemed to be emerging in her mind, with his every thrust and movement, a voice was sounding, a bell tolling, a knowledge forming that she couldn't quite grasp but knew better than to ignore.

It was all too hard to capture though. Passion was driving logic from her mind and as he moved, she pressed her nails into his shoulders, ran her fingers down his back, dug her heels into his spine for better purchase and then with a sound of frustration she rolled, moving him to his back so she was on top, in control, taking him in and arching, every part of her rejoicing in all of this, in all the perfection and pleasure that came from being with the man that she loved.

And there it was.

As pleasure exploded through her and she felt all the pieces of her fall apart at the seams, her brain forced comprehension to dawn on Amelia, so finally she understood exactly what her mother had been talking about that morning.

She loved him.

It had happened perhaps immediately, or maybe that had just been lust, but without Amelia realising what was going on, without her understanding the basis for her behaviours, and in contravention of everything she'd promised Benedetto, she realised it had all been about love.

That was why she'd felt panic at the thought of leaving him in Crete.

That was why she'd stayed. Because loving him made her brave and powerful, because, whether he was with her or not, knowing that she loved him made her strong, and whole. She hated the concept of needing any other person to be whole; she'd certainly never felt it before. It wasn't that she'd been lacking in anything prior so much as, having met Benedetto now, she realised she would never be complete without him.

And the thought terrified her, because it was the exact opposite of what he'd said he wanted, what he felt about life and relationships and his future. How many times had he reminded her that this was just sex? That he was leaving after the wedding?

'Amelia?' His voice was raspy, his own explosion having coincided with hers, so his chest was racked with heavy, sharp breaths but his eyes were watchful, contemplative. 'Are you okay?'

What choice did she have but to answer that she was? She couldn't tell him how she felt. At least, not yet. The realisation was so fresh for her, Amelia needed time to interpret her feelings, to be sure she wasn't imagining this, because of her conversation with her mother.

There was no sense complicating everything, and before the wedding, when it might turn out to be nothing.

She smiled at him brightly, collapsed onto the bed beside him and stared up at the ceiling. 'I'm glad you came to see me.'

'As am I.' He caught her hand, lifted it to his lips. 'Anton was hard on you today.'

'He always is.'

Benedetto frowned. 'I didn't realise. In the past, when he's mentioned you—'

'You saw it from his perspective,' she said with a lift of one shoulder, then pushed up onto her elbow to see him better. 'That's because you're a very good friend.'

'As he has been, to me.' He hesitated. 'I didn't like the way he spoke to you.'

Her heart lifted. She cleared her throat. 'Why is that?'

'Because you don't deserve it.' He responded so quickly, she knew the answer was honest. 'It's not fair.'

'Ah. So your sense of justice is offended on my behalf?'

'You're laughing at me?'

'No.' She leaned forward, brushed his lips with her own. 'I just thought you might be being defensive of me, that's all. I don't think I've ever had a man, or anyone, be like that. I kind of like it.'

He frowned, and she realised she'd gone too far. 'You don't need me—or anyone—defending you. You are more than capable of defending yourself brilliantly.' He kissed her back.

Her heart thundered and she felt the sting of tears cloying at the back of her throat, but she pushed them aside. There would be time to understand her feelings later. For now, she just wanted to feel, and no one made her feel better, physically, than Benedetto.

He hadn't intended to stay the night. Not because he didn't want to, but because there was a greater potential for discovery if they started acting like that and they both knew this had to be kept secret.

Or was it, he wondered, early the next morning as he lay

awake beside Amelia, naked and reluctant to leave her bed, that he didn't know how to define this, even to himself?

He'd known for as long as he could remember what he didn't want in life.

Even as a boy, he'd formed the strongest belief in a need to be on his own, never to put his life, heart, future in anyone else's hands, because that was where true happiness and freedom lay. And then Sasha had come along, and he'd experienced the wonder of loving someone—and the intense, awful vulnerability of losing them, and every lesson he'd ever learned as a child had rammed back into him at warp speed.

Nothing with Amelia changed his feelings on this score. If anything, she'd reinforced them all over again, because she was the one person he'd ever met he actually perceived as a threat.

She threatened him, with her very existence.

She made him vulnerable, just by being her.

Because if he let himself, he could really come to care for her. Not as he did now—as someone he felt protective of, someone he was incredibly attracted to—but as someone he simply wanted in his life.

The thought had him standing, pacing to the window, stark naked and unconcerned with his nudity, his gait long and athletic, as if the adrenaline coursing through his veins had energised him.

There was risk here, the kind of risk he usually avoided like the plague. With a spine of steel, and panic surging in his gut, he reminded himself how temporary this was. He was leaving, just as soon as the wedding was over. And yet, even the thought of that turned his blood to ice. Which only served to underscore the urgency of his departure.

'Good morning.'

Her voice wrapped around him like tendrils of silk, sending unwelcome sensations through his body and into his bones.

He turned slowly, steeling himself to look at her. 'Hello.'

She sat up, the sheet falling to her waist, revealing her beautiful breasts. Good intentions be damned, he prowled back to the bed like a bee drawn to a wildflower.

'You stayed.' She smiled, putting a hand to his chest, fingers splayed wide.

'I didn't mean to.' The words were unintentionally curt. 'I fell asleep.'

'I'm glad.'

'Are you?'

'Sure.' She pressed a kiss to his lips. 'This is my favourite way to wake up.'

He groaned inwardly. This was getting way out of hand. The sooner he left Catarno, the better. They both needed to get on with their lives and forget this had ever happened.

'What will you do, after the wedding?'

The question, as she sipped her strong black coffee, caught her so completely by surprise that her hand trembled and coffee spilled down her front. She swore softly, grabbing a napkin and dabbing at her robe. Benedetto reached over to do the same, but she batted his hand away.

'I'm fine. Just clumsy.' She replaced the cup carefully. 'Why do you ask?' Her pulse was racing, her heart bursting with such an intense hope she found it difficult to speak. Her insides seemed to be bouncing around all over the place.

'No reason,' he responded with nonchalance, sipping his

own coffee in a far more successful manner. 'I'm going to fly out to Athens the following morning, spend a couple of days in my office there, then move on to New York. My boat, however, is still here, and can be put at your disposal, if you'd like to use it to get back to Spain.'

Amelia reached for the coffee cup so her hands would have something to do, so she could focus on something other than his words. There was nothing new here. He'd said again and again that he was leaving after the wedding, but that was so soon now, and she hated the thought of it. She forced a bright smile to her face. 'I hadn't really thought about it.'

She stood up abruptly, aware that she was acting strangely, that she was probably revealing far too much of her feelings and not able to care.

'You don't want to return to Valencia?'

'To do what?' she asked. 'Is there any point in running away again?'

'You had built a life for yourself.'

She nodded, digging her nails into her palms in an effort to control her rioting emotions.

'So you plan to remain here?'

She turned to face him, the sun streaming in through the window behind her, highlighting her hair with natural gold.

'What's in New York?' she asked instead, staring at him as though he were a stranger. Twenty minutes ago, they'd been making love as though they were one another's salvation, their reason for being, and now he was calmly discussing exiting stage left of her life in two days' time.

'A company I'm buying. I'll be there six months or so.' *You should come visit.*

She waited for the invitation. Waited for him to say

something, anything, that might suggest he was leaving the door open to something more happening between them. Even after his insistence that this was just sex, she hoped against hope, and it was then that she understood how desperately she really did love him. And how important it was to hide that from him.

CHAPTER ELEVEN

'AMELIA?'

Later that day she blinked across at her mother, realised she was probably scowling and tried to school her features into something resembling an expression of calm.

'Yes?'

'Something is troubling you.'

Amelia looked beyond her mother, to the window through which there was a view of the street beyond the palace. Crowds had been forming for days now, lining up with flowers and fake crowns and flags, all waiting out in the summer sun to wave and catch a glimpse of the family as they left for the ceremony. By order of the King and Queen, in deference to the heat, guards had regularly been handing out water and ice lollies—but nothing was getting in the way of the festive spirit below.

Amelia wondered, if she were to move close enough, if some of that spirit might not rub off on her.

'Amelia? Talk to me,' Anna-Maria implored. 'You hold so much inside yourself,' she said, moving to stand beside her daughter. 'You are like a closed book sometimes. I wish you would open up to me. I wish you would let me help.'

Amelia compressed her lips. 'I can't.'

'Why not?'

Amelia closed her eyes, the tangle of emotions in her chest rolling painfully through her. She couldn't talk about Benedetto. It was too new, too fresh, too confusing. She couldn't make sense of it herself, so how could she explain anything to her mother?

But there was the other matter that had been plaguing Amelia since her return: her reason for leaving, her mother's choices, and Amelia's place in the family. How could she plan her future without understanding more about her past?

'Mum,' she said on a soft sigh, moving back to the table, curving her hands around a chair, bracing herself. 'There's no easy way to say this.'

Anna-Maria paled. 'You're leaving again.'

Amelia shook her head. 'No. Yes. I don't know.'

Anna-Maria nodded but her lip trembled slightly.

Frustration, shame, pity, love, worry. So many emotions bubbled through Amelia, she found it impossible to contain them. 'I need to tell you something.' And as soon as she said it, she knew she was right. She couldn't keep running from this. The threat that Daniel might reveal something was still out there, but it was more than that. Amelia needed to be honest with her mother.

Amelia sucked in a deep breath. 'Please understand, I'm not bringing this up to hurt you.'

Anna-Maria became very still, watchful.

'I know.'

Anna-Maria's expression didn't shift.

'I know you had an affair.' She dug her fingernails into her palms. 'I know he's not my real father.'

Anna-Maria lifted a hand to her lips. 'Oh, Amelia.' She closed her eyes, her face pale. 'This is why you left?'

'In part.'

'How did you find out?'

'That's not important.'

'It is to me.'

'Because you want to stop other people from finding out?' Amelia asked, the words hollow. She was angry with her mother but also guilty for betraying this secret to someone so untrustworthy.

'I found a photo and a letter. In a book in the attic. It was an accident but as soon as I saw it, I knew...'

Anna-Maria's hand fluttered to her mouth again. 'I thought I had destroyed everything.' She shook her head. 'You shouldn't have found out that way.'

'No, damn it, I shouldn't. I felt as though I'd been shot. How could you keep this from me?' She stood, frustrated. 'But it gets worse, Mum.' And now she'd started, she couldn't stop. 'I did something when I found out, something I shouldn't have done, and I—Oh, God.' She pressed her hands to her face. 'This is all such a mess.'

'Darling, darling.' Anna-Maria rushed to her daughter. 'What is it?'

'I told someone,' she whispered, scrunching up her face. 'Someone I thought I could trust. A boy I'd been seeing. I thought we were in love...'

'Daniel?' Anna-Maria asked, plucking the name from the recesses of her mind.

Amelia nodded. 'He blackmailed me. He has the DNA proof—'

'What DNA proof?' Anna-Maria asked, scandalised.

Amelia flushed. 'I got him to help me run a test.' She groaned. 'I thought I could trust him.'

Anna-Maria nodded without betraying any emotion.

'He said if I didn't pay him, he'd go to the press.'

'And so you ran away?'

'I paid him off first,' Amelia said. 'But I didn't think he was going to let it go so easily. I got scared. And I was so angry with you, and everything was so confusing, I just needed to get away. I couldn't be here, knowing my whole life is a lie...'

'It is *not* a lie,' Anna-Maria denied swiftly, urgently. 'The King is your father. In all the ways that matter, he is your father.' Anna-Maria pressed a hand to Amelia's cheek. 'Do you remember I told you about your father and me, how something happened to make me realise how much I loved him?'

Amelia nodded.

'That something was you. I was unhappy, darling, when the boys were younger. So was your father. We hadn't yet learned how to be together. I was young and foolish and when another man flirted with me, I was flattered and allowed my ego to tempt me. It was a brief, meaningless affair, and we both knew that. It was over almost before it began. But when I discovered I was pregnant, and your father couldn't have been the King, owing to his travel arrangements, I realised how stupid I'd been. What I'd put in jeopardy! And I realised then how much I loved him. I could not bear the thought of losing him, of embarrassing him, of ruining our family.' She sucked in a deep, shaking breath. 'But nor could I bear the thought of lying to him. Realising I loved him meant I needed to start our marriage with a clean slate, and so I told him everything. Everything.'

Amelia stared at her mother. *This* she hadn't expected. 'What did he say?'

'Nothing, immediately. He left the palace, for three nights, and they were the worst nights of my life, believe me, until you disappeared,' she added, shaking her head. 'But he came back to me, and, Amelia, if I hadn't already loved him, I would have fallen for him in that moment. Do you know what he did?'

'What?'

'He apologised to me. Your father apologised to me. For my infidelity! He blamed himself. He'd been ignoring me, he hadn't known, hadn't understood, how he felt for me either. He had seen that I was unhappy, but hadn't realised he could improve things for me. He said that if I would give him another chance, he would grab it with both hands. That he would love you exactly as he did the boys, perhaps even more, because you were the catalyst for us turning this corner. He was not angry. He was not threatened. And he has not once, not one day since, brought up my affair. He has never shown any hint of resenting me, of blaming me, of regretting the choice we made that night.'

Anna-Maria leaned closer, tilting her tear-stained face towards Amelia's. 'And what's more, he has loved you. Every day of your life, he has loved you. To him, you are his biological child. That's all that matters, isn't it? What's in a person's heart?'

Amelia bit down on her lip. Tears filled her own eyes, and love exploded in her heart, but it was more complicated for Amelia still. 'I'm different from everyone,' she said, shrugging. 'Half of me is made up of a man I never knew, a man who died before I could meet him, who didn't even want to meet me.'

'Yes,' Anna-Maria conceded. 'But all of you was shaped by your father. Your philosophies, your humour, your strength, your determination. These are things your father has taught you, by being in your life.'

Amelia closed her eyes, nodded.

'Oh, my darling. I'm so sorry you have carried this burden on your own for so long.' She shook her head. 'I'm even more sorry that you paid off that bastard.'

'What should I have done? I couldn't risk this coming out.'

'Why not?' Anna-Maria demanded defiantly. 'We are not ashamed, Amelia. We are not scared. You are our child—in our hearts, we know that.'

'But your affair—'

'Was a mistake, a lifetime ago.'

'I know. I just thought— I wanted to protect you all. I was scared.'

'Amelia, listen to me. Your father is not the only person to know about this. At the time, we recognised there was a risk of discovery. We have notified a select handful of people, including the president of the royal guard, the prime minister's office and a team of lawyers, engaged for just such a circumstance as this. But the most important thing for you to understand is that we love you. We always have and always will. We considered you to be a gift from heaven, and you have always been exactly that to us.'

It was purely by chance that the first person Amelia should see, when leaving her mother's suite, was Benedetto. And that he should be alone, for just about the first time since arriving in Catarno.

Amelia's heart gave a little thump before she could remind herself her heart had nothing to do with him, at least so far as he was aware. She walked towards him with the appearance of calm, his own expression impossible to read.

'Hi,' she said on a small sigh.

'Your Highness.'

Her heart trembled.

'I'm on my way to meet Anton,' he explained, though she hadn't asked.

But Amelia heard what he hadn't said: *I don't have time now.*

'Okay.' She looked up and down the corridor. People were milling about, but no one from the family, no one they knew. Still, she didn't feel she could tell him about her conversation with the Queen. Not here. 'I'll see you tonight?'

There was a beat of silence. 'I'll be with Anton,' he said. 'The night before the wedding, and all that. His groomsmen are staying in his suite.'

Amelia's heart dropped to her toes. 'Oh, right,' she said with a nod. Then, hating herself for sounding so needy, but at the same time truly needing to confide in him, 'Can you slip away briefly?'

His eyes bored into hers, and his jaw clenched visibly. It was the last thing he wanted. Her heart twisted. 'I doubt it.'

Amelia could feel tears threatening. She bit into her lower lip. 'Okay. But if you can…it's important.'

She waited for him to agree, to promise to come, but he simply smiled at her, in a way that didn't reach his eyes. 'Have a good day, Princess.'

And then he walked away.

It was almost midnight and she'd given up any hope of him coming. She knew she needed to go to sleep, or else she'd have enormous bags under her eyes that even make-up-artist wizardry couldn't disguise. But then, just as she was pulling back the covers, the small side door to her room opened and Benedetto came through.

Amelia's body responded immediately, every cell seeming to reverberate.

'Hi,' she said.

He dipped his head. 'I don't have long.'

'Anton's still awake?'

'And just getting warmed up,' Benedetto added with a grimace.

Amelia pulled a face. 'It's going to be a long night.'

'Yes.'

'I spoke to my mother,' she said quickly. 'I told her everything.'

Benedetto's brow quirked. 'Did you?'

She nodded. 'It went...well, actually.'

His jaw tightened. 'I'm glad for you, Amelia.'

But he was so cool. So formal! Her lips pulled to the side. 'We agreed not to mention anything to Dad, or Rowan and Anton, until after the wedding. But then, we'll talk to them.' She lifted one shoulder. 'No more secrets.'

Benedetto's eyes swept over Amelia's face and for a moment her heart stopped beating altogether. He looked at her with the same fierce possession she'd become used to. But he didn't move to touch her, and she wanted that so badly. 'You did the right thing.'

She nodded, awkward, and she hated that.

'And Daniel?' he prompted.

'I told her about him, too. She said they'd always been aware this might get out. They've made various high-ranking officials aware, there are contingencies in place for these sorts of things. If I hear from him again, I'll go straight to the palace police,' she said, the relief immense.

'Good.'

Silence crackled between them. Amelia felt as though

she were being dragged over hot coals. She knew it was breaking all their rules to tell him how she felt, but at the same time, having seen the truth within her heart, she knew she had to be open with him about it.

'Talking to Mum,' she started, a little unevenly, 'about her relationship with Dad, and how they fell in love, got me thinking.' She hesitated. 'About us.'

She wasn't looking directly at Benedetto but she felt him stiffen. The very air around him seemed to throb with tension, but Amelia pushed on regardless, keeping her gaze carefully averted from his face.

'Mum was saying that she fell in love with Dad slowly, and didn't even realise it for a long time, until she almost lost him—because of the affair. It was being faced with what she stood to lose that made her face up to how she felt about Dad. And it made me wonder...' Her voice trailed off, her eyes darting quickly to his face and then away again.

'Wonder what?' Benedetto prompted, not moving.

'The wedding's tomorrow.' Her mouth felt so dry, she could hardly speak. 'Are you still planning to leave afterwards?'

Silence crackled.

'Sì.'

Amelia's brow furrowed. 'Is there no part of you that wants to stay?'

'What are you really asking, Amelia?'

That was so like Benedetto, to cut right to the chase.

'The thing is,' she said, toying with her fingers, 'I didn't understand how I felt until recently. I knew you were different, that wanting you physically as I do is new for me, but on the boat it was easy to put what we were doing into a box and contain it. But here, in the real world, it's different. My feelings for you are different. Or maybe they're the same and I just understand them better.'

'Amelia.' Her name was almost a curse. She could hear his anger. 'I have told you, from the beginning, what I could offer. And what I couldn't.'

'I know.' She nodded jerkily. 'But in the beginning, we were two different people.'

'No.'

'Yes. You changed me, and I think I've changed you. I don't think you want to walk away from me.'

His jaw tightened. 'Then you don't understand me as well as you imagine.'

She ignored the pain whipping through her. 'After Daniel, I never thought I would trust anyone again. I never thought I would love anyone again. But you showed me, every day we were together, how different you are, how trustworthy and dependable, how reliable and good.'

He shook his head. 'Even if this is true, that's not love. You're just grateful I'm not going to sell your secrets to the highest bidder.'

She recoiled a little at his reductive summation. 'You knew I was a princess but you've always treated me like a woman first, a human being. You're the first person in my life to do that.'

'Exactly my point. I'm different, and that's novel for you, interesting, but it's not love.'

'Please stop trying to tell me I don't feel what I feel.'

'But you don't.' Frustration was evident in his tone. 'You've deluded yourself, maybe because you need the distraction, because you were anxious about coming home, into thinking we're in the middle of some great romance, but I've been telling you all along, it's not that. It's sex. Chemistry. And at times, friendship, yes. But not love.'

'Are you so afraid to let anyone into your heart that you would actually try to tell me I'm imagining this?' She waved her hand from her chest towards his. His eyes were unreadable; he was totally closed off to her.

'Amelia.' Again, he said her name with utter frustration. 'Don't do this.'

She flinched. 'I think you're scared.'

His throat shifted, but he didn't answer.

'You're running away, just like I did. Well, let's both stop running, Ben. Let's stop running together.'

His nostrils flared. 'You ran away; I'm just getting on with my life.'

'And you don't want me in it?'

'Amelia—'

'Say it,' she demanded fiercely, moving closer, pressing a hand to his chest, so his eyes closed at the unexpected and incendiary contact. 'Tell me you don't want me.'

He lifted a hand, cupped her cheek, looked into her eyes, and everything stopped. They existed in a vacuum and a void, just the two of them. Amelia blinked up at him, her heart bursting to explode. Couldn't he feel this? Didn't he get it?

'I want you to be happy.' He drew his thumb across her lower lip, eyes following the gesture. 'I want you to live the life of your choosing. I want you to forgive your mother and father, to find peace with your situation here.' Her heart trembled. 'But no, I don't want you.'

It was like being shot. She almost stumbled back, but held her ground, right in front of him, one cheek in his hand, her hand on his chest.

'You're a coward.' She whispered the accusation as a tear fell from the corner of her eye. Except he wasn't. He'd been through the most unimaginable grief, he'd suffered intense emotional abuse as a child, had witnessed his mother's abuse, had grown strong from that, had gone on despite it, and then he'd known the worst loss a person could live through, the death of a child, and had still managed to somehow rebuild his life, to go on, one foot in front of the other, day after day. He wasn't a coward; he was brave, but everyone had their limits.

Or maybe he simply didn't love her.

Maybe this was a fantasy, built out of her inexperience and a hopeful heart. Maybe being stranded with him in those intensely emotional circumstances had simply heightened everything.

She stared at him, waiting for him to say something, waiting for there to be more, to understand, but he didn't. He pressed a kiss to her forehead, his lips lingering there. Her eyes feathered closed as her heart surged at the contact, and then he stepped back and the world turned ice cold.

'The sooner I leave, the better. For both of us. You'll realise, once I'm gone, that this was all just make-believe.'

She wouldn't, and he was wrong, but she couldn't keep banging him over the head with the truth. She'd told him she loved him, and he'd rejected the whole idea.

'Have you ever felt like this before?' she whispered, scanning his face, needing *something*. To know that this was special, that she was different. She hated herself for asking, but if he didn't love her, at least he could admit she held a special place in his heart and mind.

'This is what I do, Amelia,' he said, the words strangely

weighted. 'I have short-term relationships and then I move on. That's the life I have chosen; it's the life I want. And not once have I lied to you about that.'

It was a form of torture. She took a step backwards, reeling, hating him then, as much as she loved him. 'So you feel this for every woman you sleep with?' she demanded.

'I'm not going to talk about my private life in this context.'

'God, Ben.' She wrapped her arms around her chest, shivering. 'You can't even admit I'm different, can you?'

Silence. Silence that pulsed and pulled and scratched at Amelia until she was almost completely raw.

'I'm truly sorry you feel this way,' he said, eventually, not moving.

Amelia tilted a glance at him, and her heart fairly shattered. He was the love of her life, of that she had no doubt. But he was also intractable and stubborn. He wouldn't change his mind. There was no point having this conversation—it would only hurt them both.

'You should go.'

'Amelia—'

'What?' She whipped around to face him, almost at breaking point. 'What more is there to say? I love you. You don't love me. You're the single most important person I've ever met in my life; I'm nothing to you. Is that a fair summation?'

A muscle throbbed in his jaw as he stared across at her. 'I don't know what you want me to say.'

'Yes, you do,' she whispered. 'But you're right, this isn't your fault; you've never lied to me. Not even now.' Her lips twisted in an awful approximation of a smile. 'Thanks for your honesty, at least.'

'I'm sorry.'

'Don't.' She shook her head. 'Don't apologise. You've done nothing wrong.' She pulled her hair over one shoulder. 'This was all my fault. My mistake.'

His eyes bored into hers, long and hard.

'I didn't mean to fall in love with you. I really thought I could control this. I thought, after Daniel, I was safe from ever feeling anything like this for anyone...' She blinked quickly to stem the threat of tears. 'Please just go, Ben. There's nothing more to say.'

Yet he lingered, watching her, and her nerves stretched and stretched until she couldn't take it any more.

'Go,' she shouted, pointing to the door, finally wiping at her eye just as a tear fell. 'I need to be alone.'

He hesitated before nodding once. 'Goodnight, Your Highness.'

She waited until the door was closed before letting go of the sob that was heavy in her chest.

Benedetto didn't go straight back to Anton's room. How the hell could he after that? He strode through the palace, his face a thundercloud, his body tense, as though preparing for war, his heart ramming against his ribs as though he'd run a marathon. He exited through a side door, found his way to a courtyard and moved to the edge of it, stood with his hands on his hips, staring out at the lights of the city, unseeing.

She loved him.

The world seemed to stop spinning. Sweat beaded on

his brow. It was his worst nightmare. It was everything he didn't want.

What a fool he'd been, to think he could become involved with someone like Amelia and not have it get complicated.

She was so different from the women he usually slept with. Amelia wasn't sophisticated and experienced, she wasn't looking for a few nights of passion and then to move on. What was worse: she'd been in an intensely vulnerable position when they'd met.

He dragged a hand through his hair.

He'd told her at every opportunity that it was just sex, made sure she understood that he didn't do commitment and relationships. He'd been so honest and upfront about that, but what did that matter?

Wasn't the reason for his constant reminders to Amelia that he knew there was risk with her? That she was so different she wouldn't be capable of understanding, truly understanding, the way he chose to live his life?

She'd had her heart broken, her trust shattered, and had chosen to stay alone afterwards, but Amelia's heart was too good to be permanently on ice. She had too much love to give to withhold it for ever.

Whereas Benedetto had been broken in a way from which he would never recover. His heart belonged to Sasha, and always would. How could he allow it to beat for anyone else, knowing what would happen if he were to lose that person too?

He clenched his hands into fists by his sides.

He'd done the right thing by holding firm in the face of Amelia's declaration, but that didn't make it any easier. And it didn't mean he felt like less of an A-grade bastard.

The sooner the wedding was over and he could leave this country, the better. Then they could both start getting on with their lives and forgetting this had ever happened.

CHAPTER TWELVE

AMELIA WALKED BEHIND VANESSA, holding the elaborate train of her dress, her features serene and impenetrable, her eyes focused on nothing and no one, even as Benedetto stared at her and willed her to look his way.

She didn't.

She wouldn't.

Her gaze was angled steadily ahead, her eyes on the front of the church.

She looked beautiful, but Benedetto could see beyond her mask, to the grey beneath her eyes, the tightening around her lips, and he knew he was the cause of that.

Had she not been able to sleep, in the same way he couldn't sleep?

Had she replayed their conversation with the same sense of frustration, because it was the exact opposite of how she wanted things to end between them?

Benedetto had known he would leave, but he had hoped they could part on good terms. That they could both look back on their time warmly.

Warmly?

How insipid, he thought with growing frustration. Suddenly, he wanted the entire congregation gone. He wanted to scoop Amelia up and take her somewhere private, with just the two of them. He wanted to be alone with her again, to finish the conversation, but to do it better this time.

Better how? What would he say? That she was special? Different? And give her false hope that their relationship might have a future after all? The more special and different she was, the more Benedetto wanted to run from her.

Her eyes flicked to Anton, and Benedetto narrowed his gaze, needing her to look at him so he could pierce her with his eyes, to smile at him and reassure him that she was already feeling better, but she didn't. Her eyes stayed on Anton's face, a smile crossed her lips—but not a smile like Benedetto had seen her give. This was practised and poised. A smile for the cameras, he thought, because the wedding was being televised. And of course Amelia, having grown up in the spotlight, was all too aware of not putting a foot wrong. She was totally in control of herself, in complete command of her emotions, outwardly at least.

She was an impeccable, beautiful princess.

His chest felt as though a load of cement were pressing down on it; his gut churned. He blinked it away, ignoring those feelings, ignoring the questions in the back of his mind. He had no doubt that leaving was the right thing, but he'd never wanted to defy his instincts more.

It had been the performance of a lifetime.

Amelia's cheeks hurt from smiling, when inside her heart was torn to shreds. She had stood beside her new sister-in-law throughout the proceedings, as Anton and Vanessa had declared their love for one another, as they had pledged to live and love for the rest of their lives, to honour and respect, and she'd known that only a few feet away from her was the only man she'd ever want to say those same words to, to make those same promises to, and yet he didn't want her. The knowledge had been like a hammer in her head and heart throughout the entire wedding. Somehow, she'd kept her cool, listening as the words were spoken, smile pinned in place, and when, from time to time, her eyes had sheened with tears, she'd known it didn't matter, because people would presume they were tears of happiness, instead of what they really were: an expression of absolute dejection.

Outside the chapel, everyone was full of joy, and Vanessa and Anton were the stars of the show, the couple everyone was looking at and adoring, so it was easy for Amelia to slip away a moment, to step through a narrow opening at the side of the ancient church and find her way through a path to a small courtyard with a fountain at the centre and a seat at the edge.

Checking the seat was clean, she sat down, and stared across the courtyard at the stone wall, eyes misting over.

She was tired. Exhausted. The act of a lifetime had cost her. She just wanted to curl up into a ball and sleep. Her eyes traced the old grout lines between the stones, seeking calm in its disordered sense, in the way the stones differed in sizes and shapes yet still somehow made up uniform lines. It was a warm day. She stretched her legs out in front of her, so the sun caught them in a triangle formed by the shape of the walls surrounding her, and she closed her eyes, trying to be still, to calm her racing mind and aching heart.

He was leaving.

There was nothing to be done about it, no more she could say, no further argument she could make. It was his life, his choice, and when she'd offered herself to him, all of herself, he'd politely, steadfastly declined. He didn't love her.

Except, she couldn't quite believe that. He'd said it, he'd been so confident, but, in her heart, Amelia suspected a love like she felt couldn't exist without reciprocation. It had been born from what they shared, from the way they'd made love, the secrets they'd revealed, the deep, abiding trust they'd built, the care they had for one another. For a brief time, all too brief, she'd walked in lock step with another person. For the first time in her life, she'd had a true partner.

What did her hopes and beliefs matter though? He'd been adamant. He didn't love her.

With a heaviness in her gut, she prepared to open her eyes and become Princess Amelia once more, to rejoin the wedding and the festivities. She sighed, then blinked, because she was no longer alone. Benedetto stood across the courtyard, in his stunning suit, looking too gorgeous to bear, and the last vestiges of Amelia's heart splintered and cracked. She was preparing to resume her act, she just wasn't quite ready yet.

Quickly she stood, turned away from him, did her best to assume the mask she knew she had to wear.

'Your brother asked me to find you,' he said quietly. 'The cars are leaving.'

She didn't turn to face him. 'I'll be right there.' Damn it, her voice wobbled.

A moment later, he was at her side. 'Amelia,' he murmured, reaching out, putting his hand on hers. She flinched away.

'I'm fine.' Her chin jutted defiantly, but her eyes were moist.

'Listen, about last night—' She heard the tormented apology in his voice, and her chest seemed to split in half.

This was all about guilt, obligation, the feeling he'd done the wrong thing.

She'd imagined everything.

'There's nothing more to say.' She stared at him, and even then, she hoped. 'Is there?'

He thrust his hands into his pockets.

'You didn't lie about your feelings? What you said last night, you meant it, didn't you?'

He was quiet for a beat and then he made a gruff sound. 'Yes.'

She closed her eyes on a fresh wave of pain. 'If you care about me at all, please leave me alone. I have to get through today, tonight, I have to be what they all expect—I don't have the capacity to feel *this* and to be that.'

His eyes raked her face and then he nodded. 'Your car is ready.'

Grateful for the return to business, she spoke curtly. 'Thank you. I'll be right out.'

He left without a backwards glance.

In the morning, Amelia awoke with a sadness in her chest that was deeper and darker than any she'd known. Benedetto would leave today, and she would never be the same.

She wouldn't see him again.

He would manage that carefully, ensuring that if he visited Anton, Amelia wasn't present. She just knew he would avoid her, to avoid hurting her again, to avoid the risk of anything more happening between them.

Accepting the reality of that, knowing he was out of her life for good, was incredibly counterintuitive.

He was the love of her life, but she had to accept his decision. Suddenly, she couldn't bear to be at the palace for all of the post-wedding activities, the necessary farewells. She couldn't bear to see Benedetto again. If they were to go their separate ways, then she wanted it to be now. Like the ripping-off of a plaster, she would never see him again. It was what he wanted.

It was still early, and she suspected everyone else would be asleep after the festivities of the night before, so Amelia took advantage of the slumberous palace and dressed quickly, washing her face, pulling her hair back into a ponytail and slipping out of a side gate, moving towards the garage.

The chauffeur startled to be disturbed but rallied quickly. 'Your Highness.' He dipped his head. 'Good morning. Where would you like to go?'

'Nowhere in particular. Just…away from here for the morning.'

If he thought it was strange, he didn't reveal as much. 'The kingfishers have taken over Anemon Lake. It's supposed to be an incredible sight. Would you care to see them?'

'Yes, thank you,' she murmured with relief, slipping into the back of the car as he held open the door for her. Amelia took great pains not to look over her shoulder at the palace as the car slipped elegantly through the gates.

Benedetto hadn't been relishing the goodbye, but he had at least expected to be able to make it. He'd wanted to see her, one last time. Things between them had ended badly, and he hated that, but he still wanted to do this part, at least, properly.

Only, upon arriving at Amelia's apartment, it was to find

it deserted. A question to one of the housekeepers revealed that she was 'out'.

He waited as long as he could, but after several hours cooling his heels, it dawned on him that she considered they'd already said their farewells. That there was nothing left to say—just as she'd said, after the wedding.

She'd come to him and literally offered her heart; he'd immediately declined. Her face and eyes had shown her hurt. Her surprise. But why should she have been surprised?

His gut twisted as he strode into the sunshine-filled courtyard. With Anton on his honeymoon, and Benedetto having already issued brief farewells to the King, Queen and Rowan, there was nothing for it but to leave.

Except, as Benedetto approached his car, the door held open by a chauffeur, he hesitated, pausing, inexplicably, to look back at the palace, his eyes chasing the windows, as if he might catch a glimpse of her, even now. His hand clenched into a fist at his side.

He knew what he had to do, and yet leaving felt strangely wrong, particularly leaving without seeing her again. He stood in the triangle formed by the open car door, at war with himself.

His head said leave, but there were other parts demanding he stay.

His head won out. He'd learned that it was much safer to trust his head, and so he sat heavily in the car and looked forward, towards his own future, and a life without Amelia Moretti anywhere near it.

The emptiness was pervasive. He hadn't expected that. After all, he'd known her for only a short time, and yet arriving in New York, after a week in Athens, Benedetto couldn't ignore the heaviness in his chest any longer, the feeling that something vital was missing from his days, from his life. He disregarded the feeling. Or rather, he compartmentalised it, as he'd learned to do as a boy, boxing away the hurt, the confusion, the disappointment and fear and stacking that tightly sealed box into the recesses of his mind, allowing him to function unimpeded.

As he'd learned to do when Sasha had become sick, when she'd died, and he'd had to co-exist with the heavy, pervasive grief of having lost her.

Except Amelia had done something to that grief. When they'd spoken of Sasha, he'd smiled, because he'd remembered all the happy, good, warm things about his daughter. And sharing that with Amelia had felt so right, as if he was bringing Sasha where she belonged—into the light. He hadn't spoken of her in so long, because no one else had tempted him to, in the slightest. But with Amelia, it had all been so easy.

He buried himself in work, taking solace in the very familiar form of denial. He spent twenty hours a day at his office, becoming master of this domain again, reading and negotiating contracts, hiring staff, micromanaging every aspect of his business. And even then, she crept into his mind when he wasn't firmly concentrating on control, allowing her to slip past the guards, and fill his thoughts, his body, so he would breathe in and swear he could taste her.

'Damn it,' he cursed, in the early hours of one morning, staring out at the glittering skyline, eyes bleary from lack of sleep. But it was sleep he feared, because in sleep, the vice-like grip on his self-control was weakened. His dreams were always filled with her.

* * *

'It's not because you're different, you know,' Anton, a month after his fairy-tale wedding and having returned from his honeymoon days earlier, sat beside Amelia in the pretty sun-dappled courtyard.

She turned to face him, her face pale, features tight, eyes, unbeknownst to her, lacking all their usual light and spark.

Anton was, for a moment, worried, though he didn't show it.

'What wasn't?' she murmured.

'The reason for us clashing. It's not because you're different. In case you think that somehow I knew, all this time, that he's not your biological father.'

Her smile was mournful; she turned away from him. It was enough to alarm Anton even further. 'I didn't think that.'

'You've always been so much better than me, Amelia.'

She frowned without looking at him. Worry for his sister stirred through Anton. Why hadn't anyone told him she was like this? She was a shadow of her former self, in terms of joy and vitality. She clearly wasn't coping with being home.

'That's not true. Has Vanessa put you up to this?'

An attempt at a joke was good, but still Anton's concern grew. 'You are so much more patient, kind, wise, willing to listen to other people before making up your mind. In that sense, you are the most like Dad of all of us,' he added. 'Biology isn't everything, you know.'

'I know.' Tears sparkled on her lashes.

Anton stood, needing more answers than he was going to get from his sister. But before leaving, he reached down, put a hand on her knee. 'Is it Valencia?' he prompted. 'Are you so desperate to go back?'

She lifted her face to his, eyes hollow, so unlike the Amelia he'd grown up with. 'No.'

A simple one-word answer that told him nothing.

'Is it being here?' Anton pushed. 'Do you hate it?'

She shook her head. 'I just need time, that's all.'

He nodded, but a sense of uneasiness was spreading through him, and there was only one person he could think of to speak to, only one person he trusted with all his innermost thoughts, besides his new wife.

He reached for his phone as he strode from the courtyard, Ben's number on speed dial.

CHAPTER THIRTEEN

BENEDETTO LISTENED TO his friend with an impassive mask. Despite the fact there was no one else in his office, he didn't want to let his guard down. But his insides were far from unaffected by the phone call.

'I'm worried about her.'

'Why?'

'She's not happy.'

Benedetto gripped the phone more tightly. 'Why do you say that?'

'She's my sister. I can tell.'

Benedetto's eyes closed.

'Did she tell you anything about her life in Valencia? About what she was doing there? Is it possible she had more going on than we realised? A serious relationship? Something important she couldn't leave? But if that's the case, why not go back? No one's forcing her to be here. Did she say anything to you, Ben?'

'No.'

'I want to help her, I want her to be happy. I just don't know where to start.'

Benedetto ground his teeth together. Guilt slammed into him. He'd messed everything up.

'She's been through a lot,' Benedetto said.

'I know. But this isn't like Amelia. I've never seen her like this.'

Benedetto leaned back in his chair, his mind conjuring an image of Amelia with ease, her beautiful, happy face on the boat, her laugh, her sun-kissed smile.

'So she didn't say anything to you?'

Benedetto dragged a hand through his hair, not answering the question directly. 'In my experience, no matter the problem, time's the solution. Your sister is right. In time, she'll be herself again.'

He disconnected the call as quickly as he could, hoping he was right.

But if having Amelia permanently moored in his brain had been hard before, it was almost impossible now that he imagined her miserable. Now that he saw her face as it had been after the wedding, when he'd found her staring at the fountain as though it held the answers to the universe. He imagined her sadness and ached to draw her into his arms, to hold her, to kiss her until she smiled against his mouth, until she laughed, or cried out in ecstatic euphoria, whichever came first. He ached to swim with her, to travel with her, to simply co-exist at her side. Five weeks after he last saw Amelia, and he began to suspect he was wrong: perhaps time wasn't the answer he was looking for. So what was?

She wasn't sure why she'd come back. Only when she'd woken that morning and gone through the motions of pretending everything was fine, that her heart wasn't breaking over and over again, and her mother had asked what was on Amelia's schedule, she'd heard herself say, without putting any thought into it, 'I'm going to Crete.'

Only in uttering the words had she realised that she'd been thinking of that day with yearning for weeks now. In Crete, they'd walked hand in hand through narrow laneways, admired brightly coloured buildings, he'd picked a geranium flower and handed it to her—she still had it flattened in between the pages of a book. In Crete, she'd stopped running: from her family, but also from the love she felt for Benedetto. In Crete she'd accepted she couldn't go in a different direction from him. And even though he'd subsequently left her, the need to be back on those streets, to exist in the midst of memories that were so tangible and real, had called to her.

'Oh, lovely, darling. What will you do there?'

'I have a few things in mind,' she'd responded vaguely. 'I'll see you later today.' She'd pressed a kiss to the top of her mother's head, bowed in the vague direction of her father, then walked from the room with more purpose in her step than she'd had in over a month.

Benedetto couldn't have said if it was courage or stupidity or a strange kind of sadism that had led him to set up a news alert on Amelia's name. Morbid curiosity? Or a desire to reassure himself that she was okay? That the press wasn't hounding her as it once had? And what would he have done if that had been the case? Flown to Catarno and rescued her? As if he had any right.

Whatever his reasons, when an email came through some time after midnight with Amelia's name in the headline of the article, he stopped everything he was doing and clicked into the link, breath held, eyes furiously scanning his tablet, reading everything, before he saw the photograph of her in a familiar setting, and every part of him froze.

His finger hovered over the photograph, but that jerked the article closed. He swore, reloaded it, forced himself to look but not touch.

Princess Amelia Moretti enjoys a break at a local restaurant. That was the subtitle that accompanied the photo.

But he knew which restaurant she was at—one they'd been to together. Where they'd sat and talked, and the sun had filtered in through the window and Benedetto had felt happy and relaxed and— He frowned, searching for another word to describe the elusive emotion that had coloured every moment of that day, until she'd run away. Then he'd gone from sunshine to shadow, feeling as if he'd lost everything in the world.

Until he'd arrived at the marina and Amelia had been waiting for him, and it had been as if he could breathe again; as if everything had been restored.

There was no sunshine for him now, only a heaviness he could hardly live alongside, a true absence of pleasure in every moment.

When Sasha had died, it had been truly awful. He had grieved her because he'd had to.

This was different.

Amelia was still here, alive, well, in another country. He was separated from her by choice, which made it harder to grieve her, to accept how much he missed her.

He flicked back to the photo, studied it, looking for any kind of sign that she was doing okay. Looking at her face, trying to understand her. Listening to the photo as though he might be able to hear her speak, hear her thoughts, learn something from the picture beyond the fact that she'd gone to the restaurant in the first place.

His instincts were pulling on Benedetto, telling him to

stop fighting this, to go and see her, to talk to her, to just work everything out later, because suddenly nothing mattered more than at least being in the same room as her. He didn't know what the future held, but he knew he could no longer live at this great distance from Amelia. She was in his soul, weaved into all the fibres of his being, and he was starting to realise that she always would be.

He called Anton from the air. The conversation was brief and businesslike—the content made that a necessity.

Benedetto and Anton were men cut from the same cloth: both private, proud, not quick to trust. Neither wanted to jeopardise their friendship, but Benedetto recognised the necessity of honesty with his friend, now that he stood on the brink of—he didn't know what. But he at least needed to explain to Anton, as a courtesy, that things were more complicated than anyone had realised. That he was coming back to see Amelia, and, finally, that he needed Anton's help. In a voice that could only be described as moderately shell-shocked, Anton agreed. 'Of course I'll help. But if you hurt her, Benedetto, if you hurt her—'

Anton didn't need to finish the sentence. They both knew what was at stake.

'I'm not really in the mood.'

'Would you do it as a favour?' Vanessa asked, a smile playing about her lips that spoke of some secret or another.

Amelia sighed softly. 'Does it have to be the marina?' She hated the thought of going back there, of seeing the boats but not Benedetto's. She hated the memories that she knew would flood her, hard and fast.

'I cannot possibly go onto a naval boat at the moment.'

Vanessa leaned forward, confidingly, looking around the dining room to assure herself that they were alone. 'I already feel as though I am fighting seasickness all day and night—standing on a boat, I would be likely to be sick everywhere. Can you imagine the photographs?' She winced and concern eclipsed Amelia's feelings of self-preservation.

'Are you not well?'

'Oh, I'm very well,' Vanessa contradicted, then quite obviously pressed a hand to her still-flat stomach. 'It's the hormones.'

'Oh!' Amelia stood up, feeling her first flush of joy in a long time, truly delighted for her sister-in-law and brother. 'What wonderful news!'

Vanessa smiled. 'We're thrilled.'

'I'm sure you are. How absolutely lovely. A baby!'

'Yes,' Vanessa whispered, looking around quickly. 'But we have not yet told anyone.'

'My parents?'

'In a week or so,' Vanessa said with a nod.

Amelia was honoured that her sister-in-law had chosen to share this secret with her. 'I won't say a thing.'

'Thank you. Now, regarding the boat opening?'

'Of course I'll do it,' Amelia agreed immediately, hating the idea of a ribbon-cutting of any sort, because of the necessary publicity that would ensue, but knowing she had to rise to the occasion. She was not the same young woman she'd been when she'd fled Catarno, nor the girl before that who'd been hounded while at university and made to feel as though everything she did was wrong. Amelia had grown up a lot in the last two years, and, vitally, had learned who she was, away from the palace and her role in the royal family.

Dressed in a striking navy-blue suit with a crisp white collar, and almost at the marina, she admitted to herself that she wasn't dreading this half as much as she'd thought she might.

Until the car came to a stop and she looked around, eyes automatically gravitating towards the berth that Benedetto's boat had occupied, expecting to find it empty, only to see that *Il Galassia* was still in port.

Her chest rolled.

She felt as though she might be sick. Butterflies danced through her central nervous system and little tiny lights flickered in her eyes. She gripped the door of the car, closing her eyes and giving herself a stern talking-to. So his boat hadn't left. That meant nothing. It wasn't even necessarily the case that Benedetto's crew was on board. Perhaps they'd flown somewhere else, to do something else, leaving the boat here to be maintained until he needed it again. Or perhaps Cassidy and Christopher were on board. Perhaps if she went to them, after the opening, they'd let her step inside. To sit for a while in the underwater lounge room and remember what it had been like to spend a week with him. Maybe even to pretend that she'd slipped back in time and they were still together, on the boat.

Her heart twisted painfully and she blinked open, eyes landing on the deck again.

The car door swung open and she knew she couldn't indulge these feelings any longer. She was on display, here representing the royal family. She had a job to do, and Amelia was determined to prove to everyone how much she'd changed.

'This way, Your Highness,' one of the members of the

royal guard said, then bowed and gestured towards the docks. There was only one other boat in sight and it was not new. She looked around, wondering if perhaps there was a larger craft further out at sea that she was to be taken to.

But the guard led her, not to any naval boat, but rather towards *Il Galassia*, and each step brought more confusion, not clarity, so that when they reached the plank that led to the back of the boat, she stopped walking, memories slamming into her now, hard and fast.

'I'm sorry, there must be some mistake.'

'No, Your Highness.'

A numb sort of curiosity had her moving forwards, her mind refusing to allow her heart to hope, concentrating impossibly hard on not imagining anything, on simply walking, one step in front of the other, until she was on the boat.

The guard didn't follow. She looked around, frowning, then continued to move forward. 'Hello?' she called out. No answer.

Lips tugging to one side, she moved up the stairs, to the next deck, then around to the front of the boat, eyes widening when she saw that, instead of the pristine white deck with which she was familiar, there were tens of thousands of red rose petals scattered like a carpet, everywhere she looked.

Her eyes squeezed shut, as if to clear the image.

When she opened them, Benedetto was standing there. He wore a suit, but the jacket had been discarded and the shirt sleeves were pushed up to his elbows, one side had come untucked. He looked so incredibly good in this dishevelled state. Though he would have looked good to Amelia no matter how he presented because it was six long weeks since the wedding and every day had been filled with a yearning for Benedetto that had taken her breath away.

Nonetheless, she stayed exactly where she was, the hurt of the past impossible to ignore, and it served as a shield now, making her cautious.

'What's going on?' she asked.

Benedetto didn't move at first either and then, slowly, he crossed the deck, stopping when he was just a few feet away from her. Close enough for her to see every detail of his face, to touch him.

She crossed her arms quickly, to prevent her from doing anything quite so stupid.

'You went to Crete.'

It was the last thing she expected him to say.

'How do you even know that?'

'I saw an article.' Was she imagining the slight darkening on his cheekbones? A blush, from Benedetto? 'Why did you go back there?' His voice was so gruff.

She angled her face away, staring out at the sea, trying not to react, trying not to feel. 'Why shouldn't I?' she said, eventually, aware that she was hedging the question. 'I'm more interested in why you're here now. In what all this is about.' She gestured to the boat.

'I don't know,' he said, moving a step closer, so she flinched. She had to be strong, but she was so tired, and had missed him so much. 'Or is it that I know, and cannot put it into words?'

'Well, why don't you try?' she snapped, frustrated and in so much pain she couldn't believe it. 'Because I'm going to walk off this boat in about one minute.'

'I don't want to do this any more.'

She narrowed her eyes. 'Do what? You're the one who came back, who brought me here.'

'I mean I don't want to do this without you.' His voice was a low rumble, like thunder. 'Life. I have been miserable since I left here, miserable with missing you, wanting you, needing you, aching to talk to you, to see you, to hear you, to just be with you. I was so sure I could conquer those feelings, that it was better for me to stay away, because I don't want what you want, because you deserve better than the future I can offer you. And yet here I am, discovering that, for you, I would do anything, go anywhere, be anything.'

Amelia's lips parted in wonder and surprise, but her brain was there, quickly tamping down on her excitement, because surely there was the possibility that she was misunderstanding him in some vital way.

'I have never been in love. I've never even really witnessed it. My parents were at each other constantly. I've avoided relationships of any meaning. But you are everywhere I look, including deep down in my soul, always in my thoughts. You are in my dreams, and everything I see and do seems a little worse when you're not there to share it with. Is this love, Amelia? Is it love to crave a person to the point you would do anything to see them, just one more time? Is it love that makes me know I would give my life to save yours? Is it love to know that I could spend every minute with you for the rest of our lives and it would still never be enough? Is it love to want to protect you from any force in your life that might do you harm even when knowing you are strong enough to protect yourself? You are the best person I have ever known,' he said gruffly, cupping her face then, staring down into her eyes. 'I don't want to fight this anymore.'

She closed her eyes, inhaled him deeply, her heart exploding.

'I hate that I hurt you. I hate that it took me so long to wake up to what I was feeling. I hate that I had to hurt us both before I could see that the only future I want is one with you in the very centre of it. Most of all, I hate that when you told me how you felt, I didn't understand my own feelings enough to shout from the rooftops that I love you too.'

She pressed a hand to his chest, struggling for breath, let alone words. 'Oh, Ben,' she whispered, tears on her lashes. 'It's okay.'

'No.' He was adamant. 'It's not. I've been such a stupid, selfish bastard, and I cannot forgive myself for that. But if you are generous enough to let me back into your life, to tell me you still love and want me, then I will never give you any reason to doubt my feelings again.'

And she knew he wouldn't. 'Even that night, I didn't really doubt them,' she said. 'I knew that loving someone like I did you wasn't, couldn't be, one-sided. Every memory I have on the boat is about *us* falling in love, not just me. This is a partnership.' She reached for his hand, linked their fingers together. 'We always will be.'

'Yes,' he said with such a sound of relief that she couldn't help but smile. 'We always will be.' And in the middle of the deck, surrounded by so many rose petals she half wondered if a whole country had been denuded of flowers, Benedetto di Vassi broke the promise he'd made himself as a young boy to always be alone, and instead begged

Princess Amelia Moretti to be his other half, always and for ever.

And she agreed, in an instant.

It was much later that day, when the sun was almost gone and the stars had come out, that Benedetto explained the process that had finally brought him to heel. He told Amelia about the news alerts, about how desperately he'd sought out even the smallest hint of information about her, but that there'd been nothing—*because I was hiding out in the palace*—until the day she went to lunch, and then it had hit him like a meteor, right between the eyes.

He loved her.

He had to be with her. There was no question of choice or free will, it was simply as inevitable as breathing.

He explained to her that he'd known their relationship and happiness had to be secured but that he'd known that happiness would always be slightly lessened if it came at the cost of Anton's happiness, of their friendship. Benedetto relayed the conversation with Anton, in which he'd very succinctly explained that he'd fallen in love with Amelia and intended to propose to her, that he knew Amelia too well to ask anyone's permission for her hand in marriage— *'I'm my own person and I'm glad you understand that!'*— but that he nonetheless felt the courtesy of a heads-up was appropriate, given their friendship.

'And what did he say?'

'There were some threats,' Benedetto drawled.

Amelia laughed softly.

'But then he told me that I deserved to be happy, and so do you, and that if we can make each other happy, there would be no greater supporter of our relationship than him, except perhaps Vanessa. Apparently she suspected something was going on between us.'

'I'm not surprised. She's very observant.'

'I didn't want to ask anyone for permission but once he'd accepted how things were between us, it was like the last piece fell into place. I knew I had to do this. I just hoped, with all my heart, that I hadn't ruined things between us completely. I was so worried you would have stopped loving me. That you'd have realised you couldn't love anyone who'd put you through this.'

'I was upset,' she agreed softly. 'But I don't think love is quite so transient as that. Certainly not the love I feel for you.'

'Nor I for you,' he promised, leaning closer, pressing a kiss to her lips. She sighed happily and snuggled into his arms.

Royal tradition dictated that Amelia should have a full, elaborate wedding, and so she did, but twenty-four hours before the ceremony the world was invited to attend via the news cameras positioned throughout the abbey, Amelia and Benedetto said their own vows privately on the deck of his boat, surrounded only by her family, and Cassidy and Christopher. It was an intimate ceremony imbued with all the love they felt for one another, and each and every guest in attendance felt that heavy in the air—it was an evening of magic, of love, and of happily ever after, just as the bride and groom deserved.

EPILOGUE

Six years later

'THEY'RE GOING TO get someone killed.' Vanessa groaned, pressing a hand to her forehead, and earning a laugh from Amelia.

'Nonsense. Teeth might go missing though,' she said, as their two oldest children—a pair of boys born only a year apart and so alike they were sometimes mistaken for twins—tore through the palace garden, a tangle of legs and arms and high-pitched laughter as they raced for the big oak tree, to see who could touch it first.

'I can't bear to watch,' Vanessa said, reaching for her tea and taking a sip.

'Then don't watch. The less we see, the better.'

'I don't know how you can be so sanguine about it.'

'I had two brothers,' Amelia pointed out.

'Hmm, that's true. I can't imagine Anton ever running around like this, though.'

'Oh, he wasn't always so boring,' Amelia responded, with a wink.

Vanessa laughed. 'You really are so bad to each other.'

Amelia lifted a hand in silent surrender. 'I'm pretty sure he started it.'

'Started what?' Anton appeared at that moment, and Vanessa's whole face showed happiness.

'Our all-out war,' Amelia joked.

'Yes, and I intend to win it,' he warned, then grinned, turning to his wife. 'The twins are awake.'

'Ah. Duty calls,' Vanessa said, standing, putting an arm around Anton's waist. 'I'll see you later?'

Amelia nodded, watching them walk away, smiling, because their happiness was so familiar to her. She sighed as she turned back to the boys, who, having reached the oak tree, were now busily trying to work out how to climb it. Even Amelia felt a slight twinge of alarm at that, but before she could intercede Benedetto was there, hoisting their son, Peter, onto his shoulders before scooping Anton and Vanessa's son into his arms and spinning him around. The laughter grew higher in pitch, and he carried them away from the tree and back to the grass, where he placed them both down and neatly pointed them in the direction of the football. It worked—for now.

Amelia exhaled a sigh of relief, then a sigh of something else, something delightfully warm and intoxicating, as her husband drew closer and placed a kiss on her forehead. Her heart, as always, pumped harder, and she reached out, her hand curling into his.

'Hello.'

He squeezed her hand. 'Hello.'

'Thank you for saving them from the tree-climb adventure.'

'Saving them? I promised I'd help them build a tree house later.'

'Oh, no,' Amelia chortled. 'You'd better include safety harnesses.'

'They're more capable than you give them credit for.' He reached for a strawberry and bit into it. 'Where's Valentina?'

'She's reading with Mum and Dad.' The King and Queen had taken to the role of grandparents with aplomb. They delighted in their five grandchildren and spent as much time as possible with them. Valentina, the only granddaughter, was doted on by all.

She's so like you were! the King would marvel. *'I never thought we would be so lucky to have a chance to do this all over again.'*

And Amelia, who had never really had cause to doubt her father's love for her, felt it radiate through her.

But there was one other child who was very much a part of their world, even though she was no longer with them. Sasha was spoken of often, brought into the light by Amelia and Benedetto, particularly with their children. For Benedetto, it had been imperative for Peter and Valentina to know about their older sister, to feel connected to her, and so he told them stories about her, showed photographs, and, in doing so, he felt those last stitches of grief begin to come together in his heart.

He would never get over losing Sasha, but he knew what a privilege it was to have loved her, and to have the chance to love Peter and Valentina. Loving, it turned out, was the greatest gift he had, and he was so grateful he'd recognised that, finally.

Amelia had run away from Catarno in fear. She'd been so afraid of not belonging, of everyone discovering that she wasn't who they thought she was. She'd been afraid of her secrets being sold to the press, and, in the end, it had all been for nothing.

Daniel did not reappear in her life.

She heard, some years later, through a mutual acquaintance, that he'd moved to London and married a wealthy aristocrat's daughter. Given his primary aim seemed to be living comfortably and working little, she presumed he'd succeeded in his goals and wouldn't likely bother her again.

But if he did, she wasn't worried.

It all seemed like such a long time ago, the feelings she'd had when she'd learned of the affair totally foreign to her now. She knew exactly who she was, and where she belonged, and with whom. She didn't fear exposure—though it never came. If it had, she wouldn't have worried, because it changed nothing. She was Amelia di Vassi, a princess of Catarno, and she was happier, she suspected, than anyone else on earth.

The next morning, with their children happily installed in the palace with grandparents, cousins, aunt and uncles, as well as a team of nannies primed for the havoc of the royal children, Amelia and Benedetto kissed everyone goodbye, as had become their annual tradition, to celebrate their wedding anniversary on *Il Galassia*.

Some years, they had been able to leave for only a night, when the children were young, and that hadn't mattered because, wherever they were, their life was full of romance and love. But now, as the children were older and very comfortable staying with family, they had a whole week to look forward to. A week on the boat that had started it all, a week together, just the two of them, more in love with every day that passed, more in sync, more convinced that they were perfect for one another than they had ever been.

* * * * *

If you just couldn't put down
His Runaway Royal
then you're certain to love the other instalments
in The Diamond Club series!

Baby Worth Billions *by Lynne Graham*
Pregnant Princess Bride *by Caitlin Crews*
Greek's Forbidden Temptation *by Millie Adams*
Italian's Stolen Wife *by Lorraine Hall*
Heir Ultimatum *by Michelle Smart*
Reclaimed with a Ring *by Louise Fuller*
Stranded and Seduced *by Emmy Grayson*

Available now!